Missing You in Belmar, NJ

MICK BENNETT

Book I

Dinosaur

1

HOW TO ACCOMMODATE people—I learned that from my mother. No household detail, however small and unimportant to my father, my sisters, or me escaped Mother's eye. She oversaw conduct but made allowances to keep the peace.

My father had rituals which he believed were his secret. On weeknights just before we all sat down to dinner, he would go out the front door and behind an old shed in our backyard to take a gulp from a bottle of Powers Irish whiskey hidden in a broken ceramic drainpipe. On Saturdays Mother let him drink in the house. Weeknights and Sundays he'd visit the drainpipe.

Once he was outside, as her serrated knife sawed through the center of two frozen blocks of peas, she would call, "I'm putting on the vegetables!" loud enough to erase the fire siren. She didn't tolerate lies so she gave him an escape route. The vegetables took ten minutes. Her voice told him he had time to drink, and then hide the whiskey on his breath with a drink from the garden hose and a cigarette.

Some secret. Our neighbor's dog knew. Hose water washed away whiskey breath. Not for me when I tried it.

A second ritual came after dark. He took walks down to the boardwalk. He always went alone and left my mother home with us children. I timed his trips. One day I borrowed my mother's watch and walked to the beach instead of riding my bike. I doubled my time and came up with my father's usual time of absence—minus seventeen minutes. Seventeen minutes over six blocks—to a ten-year-old the possibilities were endless. At first, I figured he strolled, but he was an athletic man—wiry and quick—a shade under six feet. Secret destinations came to me—places forbidden. Mother never questioned him about the walks.

She would say, "See you soon."

One night I worked up the courage to sneak out past my curfew and follow him. Man, I shook all over. No way could I let him spot me. It was mid-July, and the closer we got to the beach, the more the sidewalk filled with people. One block from Ocean Ave the streetlights along the boardwalk cast beams of welcome. He walked across Ocean Ave to the boardwalk. I stopped four or so houses short and sat on a rooming house step. He walked right up to the old pavilion—a white-columned monster looking west from the beach. The boardwalk ran alongside and behind it. Bright yellow bulbs shown under WW I helmet-shaped lamps, and inside white light filled a ballroom stacked with folding wooden chairs.

My father disappeared into the front entrance. I had to get closer, but I sure as hell didn't want him to catch me, so I waited until I could get lost in a group of teenagers crossing the boards. A milkshake mixed inside me. Everything seemed bright as noon, and the noise of voices coming from every direction moved me closer to the pavilion wall. When I turned around the northeast corner, I saw Dad.

He sat on a bench facing the ocean, arms stretched over on the bench's back. His legs spread out straight. Smoke rose from his head. My mother tolerated cigarettes but loathed cigar smoke, and for the first time, I saw a fat, black cigar pinched between my father's teeth. He wouldn't take it out of his mouth. He chewed and puffed and looked out at the water. Finally, he grasped the cigar between two fingers and flicked it. An inch of ash blew back, split, and rolled on the boards like tumbleweeds.

When he finished and stood up, I ran to beat him across Ocean Ave and home. I went in the back door, puffing, sweaty. I leaned against the mudroom wall and felt my legs go rubbery. Five seconds later, there was Mother.

"You're grounded Saturday. If your father knows, it'll be more." I rolled with it. For her accommodating secrets was child's play. Years later, she never told a soul she surprised Denny Sullivan and me. The peace of the household depended upon her.

My father had been an All-Star pitcher for perhaps St. Rose's best team ever—they won the state title his junior year. He still holds the school record for most strikeouts for both career and single season. As a freshman, he led the varsity in wins. According to newspaper clippings, he chucked so fast a batter had to sit dead red, and then in his sophomore year his curveball turned into a real yakker. Major League scouts began sniffing around. By senior year, they were at every game with their notepads. Sean made the Asbury Park Press sports pages all spring that year, even after the season ended.

That spring Miss Meagan Kinney accompanied him to the prom. Just before graduation, Sean must have been salivating. A scout could sign him when he had a diploma. He never signed with anybody. Sean and Meagan married in June, and six months later Teresa made her debut. When Mary Ellen came along, everybody worried about the war in Europe. I showed up a week before Pearl Harbor. Five years after me came Mary Jean. Mother called her "Our miracle."

Sean joined the service but never went overseas. Two atomic bombs settled his service time. After that, he became what they used to call a handy man—odd jobs from roofing to small gas engine repairs. When TVs came around, he went to school and learned all about them. I remember in the fifties he'd come home with his fat, black kit that opened like a suitcase. It was full of tubes—big ones and little ones in orange boxes with numbers printed on the ends. My father repaired something not found in his own home.

We lived in a little house on Waterfront Ave on the west side of F Street. In the summer when we had neighbors over—it only took about ten people to fill our backyard—cigarette smoke hung in the thick humidity right along with the smoke from our deluxe barbeque with a handle that turned and blew air from under and up through the coals.

Whiskey in one hand, cigarette in his mouth, Sean would crank that handle as if sounding an air raid. Sparks and ash shot up until Mother would suggest, "No one likes soot on their burger."

I fell in love with Mickey Mantle and the New York Yankees from magazine photographs and newspapers. Dad didn't share my feelings.

"An overpaid draft dodger," he called Mickey. "He'd hit lefty off me, and with that uppercut I'd hang his ass out to dry. Curves in the dirt all day."

I went through Little League and Babe Ruth. Dad came to every game. He'd stand behind the wire backstop in front of the stands. I tried to knock every pitch over the fence just like Mickey.

"You're swinging too hard," he would say.

He spoke in his homily voice from the kitchen table—not loud or scolding—just a simple statement of fact from a position of authority. Marriage is a sacrament. God will forgive you. You're swinging too hard. He didn't say it too often, but I heard it every pitch.

In his presence I had a simple, silent respect—mass without the incense, bells, and Latin. Sean Hanlon's nave was the kitchen, his trinity whiskey, questions, and cigarettes. For hymns a flicked matchbook skipped atop our kitchen table from right hand to left and back.

On Fridays, he called his family to confession. One at a time, we sat in the dark across the kitchen table from him. First, my mother, Meagan, was asked about the household money, which she managed. Then my two older sisters, Teresa and Mary Ellen, about their boyfriends or school, and I about my future. The old man ran out of steam by the time Mary Jean came along.

Sometimes Mary Ellen hid and cried, and Teresa, being the oldest and wisest, called one of her many boyfriends to come get her the hell away from the house. Teresa never dated boys who didn't own a reliable car. Sometimes it felt like Sean just warmed up on Teresa and Mary Ellen.

He saved his best stuff—his high heat and nasty, twelve-to-six curve—for me after I graduated from high school. His kitchen liturgies made it clear he wanted me out and on my own. I tooled around in a '55 Chevy two-tone and hung out with Denny Sullivan. We worked for the DPW, borough of Belmar. Denny and I were tan, blond, and free. We shared everything until that afternoon Mother discovered I forgot to lock my door.

Right after the '61 Series—the year of the M&M Boys—my father was diagnosed with lung cancer. He died before I married Sophie.

The house on Waterfront was sold, and my mother took the 'Marys' with her to Cape May County—Teresa had her own brood by then up in Bernardsville. Mother and the Marys used the money from the house and Sean's pension and Social Security to start a little craft shop. Mary Ellen did the crafts, Mary Jean did the floor work, and Mother kept the books. She passed nine years ago in 1978. By then both Marys were married. They saw to Mother's needs in the end. At the time, I lived in California. Mom is buried in Tinton Falls right next to Dad.

I remember one night after my father received his diagnosis. He called me into the kitchen. I was half-asleep. He didn't say anything for a long time. Then he spoke. "You aren't interested in a burial plot. I have an option on six for any of the family who wants one. They're not together. Three are right next to each other, then three off to one side."

I sat there and watched the clock. It hung on the wall right above the table, the cord trailing down and disappearing down to the plug. I wanted to say something, but what answer could I give?

He lit a cigarette from the glow of his old one. He poured whiskey from the bottle into a shot glass. The liquid quivered at the rim. He put down the bottle, took away an open hand, and moved it to the glass. Fingers found it. He lifted the glass to sip.

"Never mind," he let out a breath. "Never mind."

It's the same in my dream. I don't say a word. I've been having it for years. I had it when I came out of the anesthesia after my surgery.

Here's the dream.

I'm still a boy. We're at the kitchen table, the old chrome-edged and red-metal top table. It's just my father and me. It's summer, and it's dark. The back door is open, the half-screen door letting in outside sounds—cars and voices. I can see his outline against the white refrigerator. When there aren't cars passing, I can hear the humming of the condenser and his breathing, the pull of his cigarette filter from his lips, the disheartened blowing out of the smoke. He turns the cigarette against the ashtray's side, sharpening its burning tip to a point before lifting it again to his mouth.

"What are you going to do?" he asks.

He always speaks as he exhales as if the words have formed in his lungs from the cigarette smoke. He asks other things. They're never specific, never a question with an easy answer to get the conversation going. Sometimes in the dream, I get angry and want to leave, but it's like a nightmare where I can't run away. I'm frozen in the chair. Other times I want to speak, to ask him why he keeps me here at this table in the dark when I have things to do. I hear my friends outside—Hank Mariucci and Kenny Blalock.

"What are you going to do with your life?"

Holding the beer bottle's neck, he slowly traces a circle with the base's edge. He moves the bottle so the tiny groves in its base rumble over the table's center crack. Then his cigarette smears in the ashtray, "What the hell's the difference?"

That's when I want to speak. That's something I can answer. He's talking about himself, about what a failure he thinks he is. But he can't see himself as I see him. I want to tell him that. It doesn't make any difference to me, Dad. It's okay; we're okay. I want to say it, but I can't. That's the one constant. In all my other dreams, I still have my speaking voice, but in this one, I can't speak a word.

2

I MET RONNY Hopkins the summer he turned thirteen. He stood a half-head taller than his friends did, and before he filled out, thinner than most of them. He wore a crew cut—butch wax on the front cowlicks—when other kids wore Beatle haircuts. I was in my mid-twenties. Sophie and I had split up.

Ronny knew the windows of my apartment uptown. Three of them in a row, smudged gray from the dust raised by F Street traffic, just above a liquor store whose sidewalk bulged and cracked—a hell of an easy place for a kid to spill a bike. He didn't know anything about me except for the fantastic stories the senior high greasers told him. Straddling their bikes, Ronny and his buddies would watch me come down my flight of wooden steps, out that faded blue door onto the sidewalk. I always had a cigar in my mouth. I'd pace, waiting to see Alice get across the street okay after school on the way to my old house—her mother's house. Of course, Ronny didn't know that.

Across from the liquor store sat a bar that seemed to be sold every three years. Each time a sign reading "Under New Management" would hang in the window. It was called John's Office Bar—the JOB. Most of the men who drank there were black. The place had front windows on either side of the door, and sometimes during the afternoon, old eyes squinted out at the street.

One day Ronny's bunch pulled their bikes up, pointed at the window, called out a racial slur and skedaddled.

A young black man in tight pants, rayon shirt and featherweights threw the door open. "You muthafuckers better go home to your mommas!"

At that time if you lived close to the railroad tracks that bordered the town along its southwest corner, chances were you weren't rich or white.

If Ronny or his friends were interested in getting a little something for a dance coming up at St. Catherine's, they came to me. The first time I met him he asked me for a half-pint of Southern Comfort.

"Your last name's Hopkins, isn't it?" I said.

"Yeah." He may as well have added "asshole" from his tone.

"Your father's Peter Hopkins. Go on," I waved a hand, "get the hell out of here. You should know better."

Ronny wanted to break through the layers. Didn't matter if it was his old man, the principal at school, or the local cops. Of course, the older he got, the more layers he found.

Ronny smiled, gave me the finger, and rode away.

The second time his friend Rotten Kid spoke up and asked for the same purchase. I knew Rotten Kid spoke for Ronny because he ordered that half-pint of Southern Comfort. Everybody else ordered a quart or two of Carling Black Label or Miller.

I remember squinting at the glare coming off chrome and windshield of a bright, white Lincoln Continental behind Rotten Kid and thinking, take that boat back to the Terrace or North Lake Drive. I had a hangover, and I told Rotten Kid I'd pick up their beer and booze for a fifty percent tip to get rid of them. Ronny came from around the corner.

"Fifty percent's okay."

I had them park their bikes behind the building in a weedy yard and took them up the back steps to my apartment. I gave them Slim Jims, and I played them some records they said sucked. After I got tired of listening to them talk about who had big tits and what cars were boss, I asked for my money. Ronny handed me two twenties for six quarts of Miller and his Southern Comfort.

"Thanks. Keep the change.

"Did your father give you this?"

"No way. My grandpa."

"What did you do to get it?"

"Asked him for it," he smiled.

At fourteen Ronny and a friend named David Roscoe shot a swan with an arrow. It went all the way through the swan's neck and stuck there. The picture blazed across the front page of the *Asbury Park Press*. The bird didn't die—that was the amazing part. People wrote letters saying things like this typifies the serious moral decay of our youth. How dare these boys attack a helpless creature that fosters beauty and a sense of community pride?

The result? The town council president at the time—Peter Hopkins—built wooden shelters on Silver Lake's island. The actual shooter was never revealed. Who killed Bobby Franks, Leopold, or Loeb? Roscoe said Ronny shot the arrow, and Ronny claimed Roscoe did it. Next time I saw Ronny I asked.

"Which one of you shot that arrow?"

He laughed, "Take a guess."

Up until a few years ago, I enjoyed hanging around bars with younger men. Sometimes that caused trouble. One summer night I banged into people at the Tropical Pub, talking loud, telling stories. A cigar ash flicked the wrong leg, an arm knocked hard into ribs once too often. Comments came quicker until a path cleared between this big-ass Avon lifeguard and me. He gave me the finger, and then waved for me to come on.

I set my drink down on a table, balanced my cigar across its rim, and straightened up with a hearty, "Fuck you."

"Better leave it alone, Jimmy," Ronny cautioned. His crew was there.

I said, "Hot shot," and followed the guy up outside through the side, exit-only door. Everybody hooted. He turned around and smiled, drawing it out as if he was on his way to being crowned king. We went outside. Then the ground rumbled up.

Ronny found me kneeling on the grass. My shoulders were hidden in a shadow, and my legs were in a slant of porch light streaming from a backyard across the way.

"If I didn't know better, I'd swear you were praying," Ronny laughed.

I heard cop sirens coming down the street. Ronny's crew took exception because they knew me, and all hell had broken loose in the bar.

Flashlights walked around. Out front in the street, car doors slammed, engines turned over. The flashlight beams shot down our little alley, then turned around as if they didn't want to find anything.

"My floating rib is sunk," I rolled onto my back.

A few days later, Ronny made sure that Avon guard sucked his meals through a straw for the next six weeks.

3

YOU'VE SEEN THE postcards—Belmar, New Jersey—the Jersey Shore. Pictures of mom and dad decked out in matching Izods, holding Junior's hands while they all wait in line with new sunburns for a fresh seafood dinner. Maybe a Ferris wheel, its cars' colored lights reaching up into the summer night stars. Or a big Victorian guesthouse, rocking chairs with drying towels on the wrap-around front porch.

Instead, picture me about five months ago on the summer solstice, walking along Mercer Ave beach in the wash up to my knees and spotting Ronny. Understand, I lost my larynx to cancer about one year ago, and if I ever went swimming, the ocean would rush down the hole in my throat—it's called a stoma—and sink me like a stone.

My operation was right after Labor Day—a hell of a way to end summer. Ronny's father died the summer before. That was also his last full summer lifeguarding in Belmar. He got himself fired for missing days last July.

After my surgery, he visited me in the hospital to smuggle some booze in after the doctor came by on his rounds. Waiting outside the door, listening, Ronny heard the doctor say, have good luck for three years, you'll live twenty.

He gave my ass a smack. "What the hell are you doing so close to the water? You looking to sink? Come on, let's get out of here and have a cocktail. Love that white jogging suit."

He smiled. A crooked one that assured you whatever he'd just gotten caught doing was all a mistake, all in good fun. He looked in lifeguard shape, tan with long, wavy dark hair, and a wicked Fu Manchu—the center tuft under his lip trimmed to a point. I never talked to anyone who saw him lose a fight.

I took my voice out of my jogging suit's pocket. I'd just bought it. I don't ordinarily have my voice on the beach, and it's rare I have it by the water. That's why I bought my suit. It has pockets galore.

"Look at this," I held out my hand to the ocean. "Who could leave?"

"The smile isn't going to work today, Jimmy. Not your smile, not your Hulk Hogan mustache."

His words made me tired, so I sat.

"That's it, plop down like a spoiled dog. You look like a white beach ball, man."

"A beach ball."

"That suit makes your arms look so small compared to your belly."

He pulled up a towel, sat alongside me, and lit a cigarette.

There was a perfect break going. It started a good 30 yards offshore, rolled in parallel and white—steady enough so if you caught the crest early, you could ride the break all the way home. Mercer Ave is like that. Hell, Ronny started guarding at twenty-one and guarded there for over ten years. On summer's first day, it looked natural for him to be there.

"You still remember everything about the beach—the bottom's shape and how it molds the break and roll of the water? You don't miss this?" I held out a hand.

"When you move your voice against your throat, you look like you're shaving with a Remington. It makes you sound like one of those take-me-to-your-leader movies from the 50's."

He picked out this girl body surfing. She was maybe sixteen, although these days it's hard to tell. He waved to her a few times.

"Hey," I hit his leg and pointed. "See him, the boyfriend? He's jealous of the way you're staring. He shouldn't be. He should be glad he has such a nice-looking girlfriend."

"Yeah, yeah, Jimmy. Let's at least head up to the boards."

I still wanted to stay put. I stared at Ronny. I always did that, as if he would change right before my eyes. He shrugged his shoulders, turned his mouth up at a corner, and looked away before hitting me with his own smile.

"I got a smile, too, except mine doesn't have holes. I could call to that girl in the surf, piss off her boyfriend—"

I cupped my hand over my eyes and looked up. "It's not the same up there."

He waited, still looking at that girl.

I gave up. "Okay, let's go. You got your way."

We went up the tide rise where the dry sand felt soft as a snowdrift. Naturally, I had to talk to every person I knew. I ran down my batteries doing all that talking. I was a pinball bouncing from one umbrella bumper to the next. Then I started coughing. I had to take the filter out of the stoma so that I could clear the mucus with a tissue.

"The idiot still smokes," Ronny muttered to an umbrella.

We made it up to the boardwalk and stopped by to talk to the gate lady. A line of lipstick headed south past one corner of her mouth. She wore Coco Chanel sunglasses and a big floppy yellow hat, which prevented her from having a prune face after all her years in the sun.

Ronny dangled my keys in front of my face. He'd picked my jumpsuit pocket. "So how about it, buddy? Come in and take a load off. Fix us a cocktail. Can I play around with your CB radio?"

For nine months, I talked to everybody who would listen to me on my radio. I wanted to practice using my new voice, my EL. A lot of people knew my handle, and when they fired up their set, they would get in touch. It was the first day of summer, and my first day on the beach in a year.

"Screw the radio. We'll talk out on my balcony."

"Anything you say, Jimmy. Come on, catch up."

The AC was on at home. We weren't inside for two minutes when I heard footsteps coming up the stairs. I sure as hell didn't expect company. I have a second-floor apartment on Mercer—it's a condo I bought six years ago with an injury settlement thanks to a kid who t-boned me at an intersection.

The footsteps turned out to be two guys I didn't know. The older guy, Frank, told me he worked for my son-in-law at his car dealership. They both wore mechanic overalls with name stencils.

I insisted they sit down and have a drink. "It's my pleasure."

The younger kid smiled at Frank and raised his eyebrows. His shirt patch read *Jerry*.

"Just one," Frank said. "Our day's not done."

"I'll do the honors. "Oh, shit," Ronny held up the bottle. "You're almost out of vodka, Jimmy."

"No."

"What? I can barely hear you. You ran your batteries down on the beach talking." He took out the bag of batteries I keep as spares in the freezer. "You think any of these are still good?"

"I can smell your machination."

"It's not my imagination. Can you hear him, Frank?"

"What's he need?"

"You don't know?" Ronny said. "He keeps batteries in the freezer, so they last longer. And he doesn't have a car. I don't either."

"So, he needs batteries." Jerry at last got the message.

"Sure. And while you're at it, since you're finishing his vodka, would you mind picking that up, too?"

I knew Ronny had bucks—he always does, but it was my stuff they were going to get. I got my wallet and pulled out a twenty, but Ronny ushered them out the door.

"We'll be here when you get back. The half-gallon of Booths is $14.99 at Buy-Rite. They have batteries, too." "The 1.75," Frank corrected.

"That's it," Ronny smiled. He shooed them to the door.

My son-in-law has never set foot inside my apartment. He forbids me to visit my granddaughters, so these guys weren't his good friends. Frank and Jerry came back in a little while with the vodka and the batteries. Waiting for a ghost, they had two drinks watching MTV with Ronny.

"Tell Bill we stopped by," Frank waved as they left. It hurt to hear my son-in-law's name.

"You are something else," I shook my head at Ronny after they left. I threw a *Sports Illustrated* at him. The pages flapped open. I went out onto the balcony. He went into the kitchen. Ice plinked into a glass.

"Expediency, Jimmy," he bellowed. "Besides, buying the batteries boosted his self-esteem. You hear me?"

Other than Alice, a human voice hadn't spoken to me in my apartment since my laryngectomy last September. Now one called. It wasn't an Irish tenor, but it sounded great.

4

I HAD A great view from my balcony. One of my favorite things to do was sit and watch the people go by. I could see the beach, the boardwalk, the parking lot of the dance bar—called the Osprey—on Pine. Since my balcony faced south, it got the sun most of the day.

This afternoon it was even better. I had company to watch with me. I waved to some kids heading for the beach. They saw me and waved back. Ronny waved and gave them a thumbs up. I was happy—I had my new batteries, and we had plenty of booze for vodka tonics.

Sipping my drink, I took notice of the sky over the houses across the street. The clouds were rushing together, getting dark. The wind picked up and carried the smell of a shower—not so much of the rain itself as the smell of salt leaving the air. Since my surgery, I'm not always sure if it's an actual smell or memory.

Soon the rain moved down the street as if coming from a sprinkler. Big drops splashed against the building's siding. Steam rose from the wet street. People with towels over their heads ran like crazy for their cars.

"That's just my luck," Ronny pointed. "Look who found me."

He pointed at a woman hopping down from the boardwalk. She took a second to arrange hair and boobs.

She waited until she crossed the street and was right under the balcony before she hollered through the rain.

"That you hiding up there, Ronny?"

"Who do we have here?" I said.

"Her name is Peggy. Peggy Blood. I saw her a couple times last week."

"Blood? Help us, my banished brother."

Ronny whispered, "Peggy has her good points, but she tries too hard. She's divorced with a daughter. Last week, when I first saw her, I felt like a flounder circling a four-barb hook."

"What are you up to, Ronny?"

"I have no idea."

"She's in the rain, for God's sake." I leaned over my railing and waved for her to come on up. I heard her shoes on my stairs. My front door slammed, and she came out to the balcony.

"Jimmy, this is Peggy."

"I've seen you around."

I stood up. "I just got back into circulation. Jimmy Hanlon. Nice to meet you. Peggy, Ronny's no gentleman." I held a hand for her to sit next to him. My balcony isn't very wide. We brushed past each other trading places.

Thick, wet hair framed her face. Maybe mid-thirties, in great shape. A tight yellow top tied in a front knot was spotted with rain. Her bare midriff and long legs were tan. White short shorts pinched out an inch of butt cheek.

Ronny stood up. He patted her inch, and she leaned into him. The top of her head didn't quite reach his chin.

"Have a drink." Ronny handed her his vodka tonic. "You could go roll a bone or two for our guest. Jimmy has good smoke."

"Saw the weed next to my batteries, did you?"

"It was right there." He sat down. "Sit down, Peggy. Relax."

"Where do you keep yourself? You haven't called."

He shrugged. "There and here. This summer I've been something of a rover. I've been at Justin Maxwell's the past few days. I get a room for a few nights and then stay with a buddy. Either way, as long as I'm mobile."

"That's a long, ridiculous excuse."

He started spinning the Holiday Inn ashtray on the tray table. He picked it up and whirled it on one finger. "I'm a barroom Harlem Globetrotter."

"There's a phone here," Peggy pointed to the wall phone inside. "There's a phone on the boardwalk," she gestured across the street. "Why can't you just say what you mean?"

"Okay, I'm sorry." He stood up with the ashtray and threw it across the street into the empty dance bar parking lot where it broke and skipped in trails across the blacktop. Heading to the kitchen, he pounded a fist on my radio table.

"What the hell," I mouthed. I followed him into the kitchen. "What the hell are you doing? Trying to get the cops up here? And keep away from my goddamn radio equipment."

"I hit the table, not your equipment. And it's a parking lot. I bet there's no glass from broken bottles." He went into the living room and paced.

"I'm rolling some bones. Go back out there with her." I got my stash out of the freezer and rolled two nice, tight numbers. I kept an eye on Ronny. He flapped his hands around, talking to Peggy. "How about dem bones?" I mouthed to myself when I finished.

Out on the balcony I tucked one bone in my pocket and handed the other to Ronny. He fired it up, and we all passed it around. Peggy looked away when I sucked the smoke into my stoma.

I blew out a cloud and smiled. "This is how it's done."

"This is dope that grows on you."

Ronny didn't say anything else for a while. Nobody did. I started watching the clouds. The underneath layer scooted east while the darker overcast just hung above it like a frozen picture.

Ronny put a hand on Peggy's arm. "Like I said. You know I don't like corners. Here's another ashtray." He put an empty Bud can on the tray table between Peggy and me. "I'm sorry about that, okay?"

He looked at the tray table with a silly grin. Peggy half smiled and waved a hand. "Fine."

"Great." Ronny stood up. They both lit cigarettes.

He leaned back against the balcony's railing. Peggy picked up a *Sports Illustrated* from the tray table and leafed through it. She stayed on each page just long enough to check its number. I went in, brought out my picture album, and slid my chair closer to Peggy's.

"You might enjoy this more." I lit a cigar. They're soaked in anisette and make my apartment smell like licorice.

I put the album down so that a flap lay on each of our laps, and away I went. After about ten minutes, Ronny tried to get my attention. "Hey, Jimmy." I didn't look up. Then, "How about that other bone, Jimmy?"

I wanted to finish my album first. My daughter came next. Still to come were the two granddaughters, the years in Miami, and the apartment in North Jersey with Alan Alda's father as a neighbor.

"Drinks? Who needs a drink?"

"I'm good. Peggy?"

"I'm good."

"This is Jack Billings. With his mother, up in Chicago—only six weeks after we all lived in Miami—they went out one night. They got drunk, slipped down on an icy sidewalk, and were found the next morning, frozen to death."

"My God," Peggy said.

"That's a lot of the living Jimmy's done. Mostly the nice. The not so nice isn't pictured. I've seen it all. Blow your cigar smoke out your hole for Peggy."

"We just met." I went back to my album. "This is where I lived up in north Jersey. Alan Alda's father lived in the same complex. Sometimes I'd fix a pitcher of martinis. He'd say, 'Jimmy, be right over.' A very fine gentleman."

It took a while to go through the album. Peggy wanted to know everything about every picture. I showed her one of Alice when Peggy mentioned that Linda, her daughter, was interested in speech therapy.

"No kidding. I sign some, and I fingerspell. I learned just in case."

I thought a wasp stung Ronny's ass. "Oh, Jeez! You ought to give her a call. She should see all of Jimmy's stuff."

"Linda has a stack of books."

"Jimmy has shelves. Give her a call. Or bring her when you come back. You're coming back later tonight, right. We can go out from here if that's okay."

Peggy smiled as if he'd just told her she could take another roll after craps.

"Okay. Can I get some water? I don't want to be drinking this bomb if I'm going out later. Sheesh. Did you wave the tonic bottle over all this vodka?"

"I make them a little strong."

Peggy made her call. It was all set. "I told Linda I'd have to scramble for dinner," she said as I showed her to the door.

I went back to the balcony. "I bet you've seen the daughter. How old is she?"

"I've seen her. Hey, how about that other bone? For later with Peggy."

"And how old is she?"

"Who?"

"Linda." I flipped him the bone.

"Peggy had her at seventeen."

I gave up.

Linda and Peggy were supposed to show up around eight—more company—I loved it. I wanted to be presentable, so I took time for a shower, shave, and nap. I gave Ronny some money, and he walked up to 7-11 and bought some sandwiches. He also picked up some milk and Coke.

To be ready for Linda I got my books together. I'm up on matters of communications, electronics, and ASL—American Sign Language. When they taught me about my electrolarynx, or EL, I was already familiar with vibration tech and what not from my radio hobby. I even suggested some improvements for the design of my EL.

I sat out on the balcony to watch for them. The shadows of the houses along Ocean Ave stretched onto the boardwalk when I spotted Peggy. Next to her, a girl was walking a bike. She hopped on it at the ramp, coasted down to the crosswalk, and peddled down the street. Her bike was a kid's bike—sky blue with white streamers. She wore a tan sundress with spaghetti straps. She looked fifteen years too old for that bike. Her massive, poofy hair could have hidden a small animal. She jumped the curb in front of me, let her bike drop onto the grass, and lit a cigarette.

Peggy, half a block away, yelled, "Why can't you wait? You don't know which door!"

"I know which building!"

When Peggy arrived, she pointed up at me, and I waved for them to come up. I went inside. "It's them. No ashtrays."

Linda came up first and went right over to my books that I set out on the kitchen table. "Are these yours?"

"Yes. I'm Jimmy."

Ronny slid alongside Linda. "What am I, chopped liva?"

"Ronny." She put a hand on his shoulder, stretched up, and kissed his cheek. "So how's it going?"

"So where are we going, Ronny?"

"Going great. How about this stuff?" Ronny picked up one of my books and opened it. "Your mom says you're really interested in this type of thing. I know some signs. Jimmy taught me." He signed beer, bullshit, and two peace signs turned opposite, thumping together. "You can guess this one."

"Yeah." She fingerspelled to me, *everybody knows that*. Then she snatched the book from Ronny's hands so fast his palms were still up.

"How about some screwdrivers?" Ronny said. He walked to the kitchen, opened the freezer, and took out ice trays. He made four, announcing, "Three regular screwdrivers and one virgin." I realized later that virgin was sacrificed the same as the other three.

I showed Peggy out onto the balcony. I could see inside. Ronny carried two screwdrivers from the kitchen. On his way to the balcony, he leaned down to Linda's ear, whispered something, and tapped his Marlboro box in his shirt pocket. Linda's eyebrows went up, but her eyes never left the book. They joined Peggy and me.

Linda wanted to hold my voice. "Mom says you call the electrolarynx your voice."

"Voice is good. Voice or EL. Electrolarynx is hard to say, and people forget." I handed it to her.

"Show Linda how you smoke, Jimmy."

Linda gave the EL the once-over. I watched her spin it around. She put it up to her throat but didn't say anything.

Peggy lit a cigarette and blew out the smoke in a huff. She fixed her hair, fussed her outfit—a white see-through shirt with a white bra underneath. Her eyes grew that four-barb stare focused right on Ronny.

When Linda finally gave me back my voice, she turned to Ronny and put her thumb and forefinger together next to her lips. She winked, and Ronny took out that bone. He looked at Peggy.

"Do you mind?" Without waiting for an answer, he fired it up.

"I mind. Hell, yes. No way."

"Come on, Ronny," I said.

Ronny took one toke and knocked off the ash against the balcony railing. He dipped the burned end in his driver and then tucked it back with his Marlboros. "Two against one."

"Don't I count?" Linda said.

"No. Are we or are we not going out?"

Ronny stood up. "Someone's put something in my drink."

"Turn that up," Linda squealed. "Oh, Lord, I love this song. Turn it up." She danced inside following Ronny. "Where is it?"

"Right here." Ronny blasted it—I had no idea of the title—but Linda grabbed Ronny's hand and began dancing. Peggy watched them. She lit a cigarette off the old one and winged the match over the balcony.

"Kids. Jimmy, it isn't easy these days."

I smiled and shook my head no. I don't bother trying to talk over loud music.

"Her father took off when she was six. The usual story."

It wasn't usual enough to keep her from telling it. She'd been going at it after she left in the afternoon from what I could gather. She had this sad, little smile that always seemed to come back after each puff she took on her cigarette. After she finally finished talking, she flipped through the book her daughter had brought out. Now, at my apartment, you can see from the balcony into the kitchen with the refrigerator door closed. But because the fridge is right inside the doorway, when its door is open, you can't. I saw that fridge door stay open for way too long with two sets of legs underneath.

I sat Linda down with my album when she wandered back. Her eyes were glassy and darted around like little BBs in plastic puzzle eyeholes. Ronny was in the bathroom. Judging from the aroma—I can still smell weed—he'd fired up that bone again.

"I'll go fix us some cheese and crackers." I went into the kitchen. I had three slices of Vermont cheddar cut when out on the balcony Linda and Peggy yelled at each other the way only mother and daughter can.

"Prove it!" Linda kept yelling.

"I don't have to prove you're drinking alcohol. I'm your goddamn mother!" She went inside. "Hopkins!"

Ronny came out of the bathroom packing his best innocent smile. "Next?" He swept a hand toward the door and bowed.

"Next my ass!"

Peggy dragged Linda by the hand. The two of them blew past him down the stairs.

Ronny and I headed for the balcony to watch the show.

Linda yelled something about going to see somebody named Tony before taking off on her bike. She hiked up that sundress to her waist. Peggy pulled off her clogs and headed for the boardwalk. She flipped the finger to anybody watching. I thought the night was over, but a few minutes later, Peggy out of sight, Linda came back from wherever she rode. She smiled up at us and dropped the bike in about the same spot.

"Look who's back," Ronny smiled. He went into the kitchen.

I should have just locked my door. Instead, I had what I call a dope-notion. I had an idea that someone could behave himself, and that someone else had been behaving. I invited her up and opened my album.

"Mom left mad." Linda plunked down next to me. "Mad at Ronny for not paying attention. Or mad at me for drinking, but I don't think so. That wasn't it. She's pissed I'm on birth control pills. I have bad periods, and so does she but she isn't. Jimmy, who is this?" She tapped a finger on a picture of Alice.

"My daughter."

"You have a daughter?"

"Alice. To daughters," I drank.

"What is that drink?"

"Vodka and tonic."

"Can I taste?"

"One sip."

"Yuk," she scrunched her face. "It tastes bitter. I like screwdrivers. Beer, too. Bud's my beer. I told Mom it sucks that you lost your voice, your real voice. Your stoma doesn't look bad." She took another sip—more of a gulp. "Oops. I taste lime. Is that the lime?"

"One of them."

"Where's your daughter live?"

I got back my drink, all vodka, and she went on like that for a few minutes before she stared down at the album as if the pictures were alive.

Mr. Hopkins returned and sat next to her with their screwdrivers.

"She's not drinking that, you asshole."

It didn't matter. After another minute of looking through the album, she excused herself and got up. She stood still for a few seconds then scrambled to the bathroom. I stood behind her while she heaved. I patted her shoulder, got a washcloth with cool water, and used it to brush hair from her forehead. When she finished, she sat back and waved a hand okay.

Just as I closed the door so she could get herself together in private, I heard a bang. Then another—my door slammed.

I went out onto the balcony. Ronny had kicked my tray table. Came up underneath and lifted the top right off that son of a bitch so nice the legs stayed on the balcony. Drinks, my album, my voice—they all went over the railing. I could see things down in the grass. I put both hands on the railing and watched him walk across the dance bar parking lot.

5

IF A RESEARCHER graphed the number of apologies during any summer, he'd have a lump of them in June and a blank space alongside Labor Day. Who apologizes at the end of summer fling? According to Ronny, apologies should serve a purpose.

I had a burn on the back of my neck, so the next morning I took a taxi up to Rite-Aid. John Beyer informed me that a certain gentleman had that morning placed an order for an electrolarynx.

He stated, "I thought you may want to know," matter of factly as he bagged my Aloe Vera lotion. The cab pulled up to my place and I saw Ronny. He had his apology set and a surprise.

"I lost it last night. Too much fire water. Peggy didn't help. What the hell, Jimmy. I'm sorry. I ordered you another—"

"I just left John Beyer."

"That was the cab, huh?"

"That was the cab."

"Come to J's with me. I have a meeting with Casivette. He wants to talk to me."

"Casivette? Are you kidding? You're a movie trailer."

"I saw him in the damn drug store. You'll keep me calm."

"I don't want to miss your coming attractions." His smile drew me out of my poor-me funk into whatever the hell's its opposite. I went with him.

J's Corner is on Brystol and Ocean Ave, one block north of my place. We sat at a picnic table outside. Ronny got a bagel; I got a *Post* and coffee. We weren't there ten minutes when John Casivette drove up in his truck and parked in a diagonal space across the street.

Casivette has overseen Belmar guards for fifteen years. About my age, to strangers he might appear too short and slight to be a guard, but he was wiry and strong—one hell of a swimmer. He always dressed in the same outfit—red guard shorts and lifeguard belt over his shoulder along with flip-flops and reflector shades. A few years ago, he decided to wear a pith helmet. He had a permanent leather tan. That combined with the zinc oxide smeared above and under his eyes made him look an escapee from a minstrel show.

"Hey, Hopkins," Casivette waved. "Over here. I got appointments."

"Like he's still my fuckin' boss, Jimmy," Ronny muttered.

Ronny went across. I followed him, walked to a bench facing Ocean Ave—the benches alternate between facing east and west—and had a seat. I wasn't going to miss this conversation. They were right in front of me, the width of the boards away.

Casivette put a foot up on the boardwalk steps and crossed wrists on his knee. "What are you doing this summer?"

"I have no idea."

"I'm in a bind till after the Fourth, Hopkins. Can you do some covering for me?"

"Correct me if I'm wrong, John. Didn't you fire me last year because I was out once too often? And now you're coming to me in a bind?"

Ronny did a Hollywood routine. He looked down, slid his shades Steve McQueen-cool to the tip of his nose, and then looked up at Casivette. Some kid rode a bicycle too fast up the boardwalk ramp and almost spilled it.

"It does intrigue me, going back to guarding. And that you're asking."

"How about it? I don't have all day. I need somebody experienced."

"Till the Fourth. What happens after?"

It was Casivette's turn to make Ronny wait. He stepped away, moved next to a parking meter, and watched cars go by. A big borough truck drove past.

He turned away from the noise. "We'll see, we'll see. Look, you play square with us, and maybe we can give you a job for the season. Okay?"

"Thirteen years on the beach, and you're treating me like a rookie. Who the hell are *we*? *You* do all the hiring and firing."

Casivette chuckled. He hopped up on the boardwalk and strutted around in little circles like a peacock in the company of crows, balancing the belt on his shoulder, toes gripping flip-flops.

"Okay. I'll give full time. You're a Lieutenant on Inlet Ave. Jim Highspire's your Captain. Under you, there's a rookie, Billy Harris, and two others, Vinny Fontana and Sam Cooper. You know those two?"

Ronny's mouth opened wide when Casivette said Inlet Ave. Here it comes I thought. That's supposed to be the beach where men in small bathing suits hang out with each other. I bit my tongue. It has quite a few scars.

"Lieutenant. At the faggot beach."

"Don't thank me." Casivette held up both hands. "Just be sure you don't let me down. Be there on time, today at two. Maybe we'll work you out, so be there sober."

He hopped down off the boards, climbed into his red pickup, and drove off.

"I'm fuckin' back!" Ronny lit a cigarette and stood next to me. He faced the ocean. "The sun feels good on my face—nothing like morning sun on your face." He grabbed the storm fence top with both hands, shook it and yelled, "My insides are up, Jimmy!"

I couldn't believe it. Full time again.

"What time is it?"

"Around eleven-thirty."

"Estel's is open. Let's go. We're celebrating."

Estel's was six blocks away on Essex. I had time to think. I tossed out several ideas for Ronny's consideration along the way.

"Casivette told you to be there sober."

"Two beers maybe."

"You're thirty-three with no permanent or temporary place to live."

"So? Come on, let's cross."

"You told me last summer you didn't recognize songs the younger guards cranked loud."

"I'll pick the stations."

At lunchtime on sunny days, Estel's is a dull bar. It has a picture window stretching across its front so you can sit and look out across Ocean Ave at the boardwalk and beach. Like lots of bars I frequented, I went through cycles at Estel's. I'd skip spring and summer after an altercation, and when I went back, the only things that changed would be some staff and the music on the jukebox.

There wasn't a soul there when we walked in. Somebody had propped the door open to let in fresh air. A cleaning service van just pulled away from the back driveway. It's funny how the smells of disinfectant and old piss can mix but never separate. The bartender—a young kid—carried cases of empties out and stocked cold bottles into the coolers.

"Kitchen open?" Ronny hit my arm. "I'd like a large pizza with anchovies and Habanero peppers."

"We don't serve food here." The kid banged in the cold bottles, packing them tight.

"No shit? Well, I've eaten. How about a couple of beers?"

Day bartenders have it tough on nice days—nobody comes around, at least not on weekdays. We got our beers. Ronny sipped his and happened to look out the window.

"Shit, look at that. The boys on Essex have a job."

For a lifeguard a job is a save. We both went to the window. Two guards were taking out the boat. People started coming off their blankets to stand along the tide rise as if they were at a ballpark.

We went out on Estel's concrete porch. It has a solid railing maybe three feet high and big square pillars. Ronny climbed onto the railing.

"It's a fucking inflatable raft—one of those two-man things with short, plastic oars. Goddamn things should be banned."

I got up there next to him. The raft had drifted way the hell past the third barrel and two idiot civilians swam toward it. Three boys rolled around in the thing trying to paddle. The more they rolled, the more it deflated. The two civilians tried to hold on to the slick plastic. One kicked and got a belly up, then pulled a kid's neck to climb in. When the guard boat arrived, everybody deserted the raft.

"Supreme stupidity at its finest," Ronny laughed.

"I'm looking at it," a voice said. It was Peggy below on the sidewalk. My first thought—shit! Did she talk to Linda about last night? I wondered because after Ronny kicked his field goal, Linda busted my balls. I hadn't told Ronny what she did. I played it dumb.

"Come up here and look at this," Ronny said.

"Why should I after last night? I should be ignoring *you*."

"Too much weed and booze. I told Jimmy sorry. Now I'm telling you. I'm sorry."

Peggy started up the stairs.

"You're not going to the guillotine." Ronny held his hand out for her. She took it, and he helped her up. She tucked strands of hair behind an ear and looked out at the circus.

"My God. Why the crowd?"

"It's nothing. Just a drifting raft. That's why I'd never work on the damn raft beach. Hope somebody's cleared the water while those clowns play out there."

Ronny held her hand as he hopped off the railing. The backs of Peggy's thighs were right in front of him.

"You have good color for June. That job's got my insides up. I'm back on the beach. Two more hours of freedom—that's all I have left. Help me celebrate. I owe you one from last night."

"Two more hours?"

He never let go of her hand as he moved a half step back and took in more of her. Her cut-offs just covered her butt, and she twisted two fingers in his hand as her weight shifted from one leg to the other. She turned her hip and stretched the opposite leg out, and he ducked his head between her legs and lifted her onto his shoulders.

"Oh! Jimmy, what the hell's in that weed?"

I didn't answer her. In Estel's she started out sitting at the bar face forward, but with every sip, she made a little swivel in Ronny's direction. After two drinks, she punched his shoulder. An hour later we all left Estel's, a few crumpled dollar bills sitting in a puddle alongside a triangle of swizzle sticks. I headed north. Peggy announced she and Ronny were going south to Chester Ave.

"Chester and C Street. You better believe I got that house. Bastard left me flat."

From her story the night before I knew she meant her ex-husband.

The clock outside J's read 1:55 when from my picnic table I spotted Ronny and a 7-11 jumbo coffee coming down the boards. I walked across to Annie, the Inlet gate lady.

"Jimmy," she gave me her hand. Annie's hand is pale and gentle. The back is small fish bones with a map of blue roads. Maybe she's fifty—she won't tell—with long, graying hair she likes to braid. She wears a sombrero with different fresh flowers from her garden tucked into its band.

Ronny pulled me away from Annie.

"Let me tell you—"

I held up a hand. "I don't need intimate details."

I got them.

"Three feet inside the door…it's wide open. Cars are going by. We're on the carpet kissing. The way she kisses. Wide, slow circles. So we're going pretty good. She's shaking her head from side to side. Then on a shiny new dime, she stops, cranes her head up and looks me in the eye. She says, "You hear something?" She smiles, gets up on her elbows, right in my face. "Is there somebody out on the porch?" But all the time, she keeps right on bucking. Doesn't miss a beat."

"Thank goodness for that."

6

I N BELMAR, BEACH gates are every block, and because so many locals wander the boardwalk to stop and talk with the gate guards, town news travels faster than a Clemente peg from right field.

I introduced Ronny to Annie. "I know about you. You're the new guard—the new old guard. Welcome."

Ronny sipped his coffee. "I thought I knew your name, but most of you ladies wear hats so big and floppy that you can't see a face. What fine work do we have here?"

Annie looked up from her cross-stitch. Ronny flashed his smile. She turned away for a second with a little more color in her cheeks.

"This is cross-stitch." She held it up. "This is going to be a Christmas scene for my niece. Over here, there's going to be a reindeer, and see the outline of the house? The thing is I can't decide where to put the chimney. That's why there are three spaces. See?"

Ronny nodded, smile locked tight in place.

Annie put a finger on the spaces at either end and in the middle of the roof. "What do you think?"

"Why not put a chimney at both ends? Two fireplaces are cozier than—oops, here comes my new boss."

Highspire jogged up the beach toward the gate. In his late twenties and more settled, he'd cheered on that Avon guard in the Tropical. Ronny knew him from way back. One summer Ronny put Highspire's back against a wall at Estel's. They worked together when Highspire started guarding, but of course, now Highspire was a Captain, and that changed everything.

"Hopkins, where the hell have you been?"

"Watch the language, High horse," Annie snapped.

Highspire completely ignored her. "At least you're here. Let's go. Or am I keeping you from a cross-stitch lesson?"

I smiled, waved good-bye to Annie, and walked onto the beach with Highspire and Ronny. Ronny walked toes-first. His choppy steps splattered sand ahead in little puffs. Highspire changed course toward a girl on a chaise about ten yards north of the Benny rope—a rope on three sides of the stand to keep people clear for equipment. I set up my chair within radio range of the stand and settled in for the show.

Ronny pointed to a kid on the stand.

"What's with the headphones?"

The kid drummed with imaginary sticks. Tanning oil winged off his arms. He didn't say a word.

"Take off the headphones!"

They dropped around his neck. The radio screamed, and he turned it down.

"I'm Hopkins, your Lieutenant."

"I'm Harris, the rookie." One of the new, young lions with buzz cut and ear stud, a husky kid, well-defined in his upper body, his shoulders stretched back in permanent attention.

Sam Cooper sat next to Harris. He was the only guard of the crew who could be called a beast. Ronny's height but thirty pounds heavier, he played defensive end in Division II football. Guarding was his summer hobby until coaching and teaching took over before Labor Day.

He slid over, and Ronny climbed up next to the kid. "Highspire lets you use headphones?"

"Nobody's in the water."

It was an empty ocean—a weekday with mostly older guys sunning behind wind screens. The water pushed against the Inlet Ave jetty in bright, choppy surges. The southeast wind kicked the surface into small swells with no clear line of breakers. Overhead clouds blocked the sun and passed a shadow over the water. It changed to slate-green, then grew bright and dark blue with the cloud's passing. On the horizon, the sky and water joined in a gray mist against the silhouette of the pleasure boats up and down the coast.

Harris turned up the radio.

Ronny grabbed it and turned it off. "What *is* this new stuff they call music?" Ronny cocked an ear east. "That noise—can you hear it? It's called the ocean."

Harris laughed.

"You expect to hear anything over this noise? Suppose there's trouble up the beach? The water's not your only responsibility. Highspire ever tell you that?"

"No."

"You're not going to hear most people yell. That shit's in the movies. Their body movements telegraph trouble first. You need to anticipate, spot potential trouble. I hear a little whisper when I see a doggy paddle past in chest-deep water."

Harris listened. He was a friendly kid. Not a drop of smart-ass in him. When he took lunch, he launched himself off the stand, landing a good ten feet out.

I looked around for Highspire and saw him kneeling, talking to the chaise girl, his red windbreaker tied around his waist California style. That's some place, California. I tended bar there for six months. It's the only time I ever heard a construction hard hat just off work order a Campari and soda.

Ronny looked content on the stand. There weren't too many people on the beach. Maybe the wind kept them home. There were two bathers with white skin, the milk-white kind that looks like it's never been out from under a suit and tie. The two tried to swim out, but the southeast wind took them five yards sideways for every yard they went out. One had a crawl like a corkscrew. He turned his head with every stroke, his arms stiff and straight, and elbows barely breaking the surface.

Highspire walked up to Ronny. "You ready for a workout? Harris gets back, we'll take you out for a little swim, okay? You've been keeping in shape, haven't you?"

"Sure. You want a urine sample? Step over here."

"Just a timed barrel swim, my man. It's Casivette's idea."

"Shit. Look, Highspire, how about if we do this test business tomorrow? I had a busy week all morning."

"Not on your life. Casivette wants your swim time today before he goes home. Who knows," Highspire smiled, "he might even be by later to watch."

Ronny had his backpack on the stand's footrest, and he reached in and took out a Marlboro. He lit up on the first match.

"Good. I hope he decides to do a line job. I hope he decides to personally assess my water skills."

"Is that so?"

Ronny stuck a thumb against one side of his nose and fired a bazooka-snot down to the sand. "You could wear oven mitts and still be a jerk-off."

"Nice to see you've changed."

"In fact, I can't wait till Casivette shows up. And if he doesn't, I'll take you instead."

"You know I can't leave just one man on the stand."

"Not even Cooper?" Ronny said. Cooper never flinched. "Let's go as soon as Harris gets back. Hey, look, Highspire. There's hardly anybody in the water. What the hell?"

Highspire had worked out with Ronny plenty. Ronny has as much buoyancy as a bone. He has long, thick arms, and in the water, he knows what he's doing.

"Okay. We go as soon as Harris is back if nobody's in the water. In the sixty-one-degree water."

"Restroom. I'll be back," Ronny hopped off the stand. I saw him grimace and make a move to touch his right knee, but he saw me watching and straightened up. "Summer's here!"

"He called your bluff," I said, but either he didn't hear me or didn't want to.

He walked to where that girl sat by herself on her chaise and stood there. Bundled up in a blue blanket, she held a book—big and thick with red thumb spots like a dictionary.

"That blanket reminds me of the one I had as a kid, except mine had white sailboats. Ronny Hopkins." He put out a hand.

The girl looked up, smiled, and took his hand. "Robin Malloy. Sloops or schooners? Are you lost? The rest room's up there."

"Nope. They were schooners. I was a divided rigs kind of kid. Much more romantic."

"Have a seat, Ronny Hopkins." She pointed to the sand. "Let me tell you something. I've been watching you. You need a change, mister. I've listened to you for about an hour and know all about you. You need to decide what you want down deep."

"Serving anything besides clichés for lunch? Mind if you tell me how you know all this?"

"Didn't I tell you? I'm a witch."

"You and Highspire friends, witch?"

"Lord, no." She turned her head. "Ah, here come my friends."

Two girls joined the party. Highspire walked over and nodded in Ronny's direction. "Harris is back. Cooper's going to lunch. You're back up top, Hopkins, with Harris. You two talking about me? My ears are burning."

Ronny stood up. "Try sunblock."

Highspire stood there with his arms crossed and talked about tides and currents, and every time he made a point, he reached down and rested a hand on Robin's shoulder. While Highspire went to town—hell, he walked down Broadway—Ronny turned around up on the stand, that smile catching the sun, and waved to Robin.

"Harris, I'm about to educate you on some of the finer points of lifeguarding. Move over. Number one—always remember that on the beach, voices carry with the wind, and disappear against it."

Casivette never did show up, and Highspire spent most of the afternoon telling Robin and her two friends everything he could think of about himself until they packed up their stuff and left as if lightning had struck. It amazed me how a man Highspire's age could be so stupid when it came to women.

I kept an eye out for Ronny from my balcony. He waved to me from the boards, and I circled an arm for him to come up. For the last nine months, I'd had eye contact with a Pharmacist, the clerks at Huxley's Liquors, and assorted doctors in white medical coats. What was I going to do? Not invite him up?

"How was your day, dear?" I held out a screwdriver for him. He smiled wall to wall. We clinked and knocked down our drivers.

"Come in the kitchen. I have stuffed chicken in the oven. Potatoes baking, too."

He came in with me. In the sink, thick white ends of celery and onion skins mixed with dirty glasses. I got rid of the organic mess, filled the sink with sudsy water, and got my sponge-octopus thing.

"Clean up before the meal. Then you can enjoy and relax afterward."

"I want a taller glass—more room." He grabbed my favorite Yankee mugs off the drain board.

"I just washed those."

"Right. That's why I'm using it. They're clean."

"By the way, what about your trip to the Keys? Now that you're working—" I started laughing—the moment plus the driver. I had to clear the phlegm before I lit up a cigar.

"You and those cigars." He put my drink down, lit a cigarette, and leaned against the wall. "You saw that girl I talked to? Robin?"

I smiled so my cigar tilted up.

"Blue blanket, blue eyes, Dorothy Hamill haircut? I saw her. You meet girls all the time. You should meet a woman."

"There you go. Fat ass, stout opinion. Listen, I talked to more people today, listened to advice, orders, *reality,* Robin spouted—"

He went out on the balcony and took some deep breaths.

I came out to him after a while. "It's an old song." I set an ashtray down on the tray table—my favorite ashtray, from the 1964 World's Fair. He looked down at it and shook his head. Then he went inside and finished up in the kitchen. Pots banged; silverware collided on the drain board.

There wasn't a sound for a while—a minute or two. Probably looking through the records, I thought. With the first few scratches, I recognized it. I didn't have to hear a note. Ronny and I both love The Four Tops, and there's a very distinct swish-crack at the beginning of their *Greatest Hits* album just before "Sugar Pie, Honey Bunch." Inside fingers snapped with the first bar, and by the time the percussion joined the piano, I was alongside snapping mine. Always a drop-snap—start with the hand at the shoulder, drop it, snap, and turn the wrist in like you're breaking off a curveball. It's the only way.

Then Ronny had the ketchup bottle for a mike; I had my voice, but I only mouthed the words because I don't like to sandpaper the music. We went all the way through both sides, drinking and turning it up full blast. We never did get to dinner.

He started to say something, but I held up my hand. "Go on, get yourself cleaned up." I switched off the turntable. "Before you do—where are you staying? You find a place?"

"No time."

"Why not stick here till you do?"

"Sure. Thanks Jimmy."

I got him some towels, a washcloth, and cologne. "Don't forget to turn on the fan." I put on the Temps— "The Way You Do the Things You Do." I'd flipped over to side two by the time Ronny left the bathroom—steam rolled out like a fog when he opened the door.

"What the hell happened to the fan? Ronny caught one wet foot in his jeans and down he went. The Temps skipped and I laughed. "You're not shaving? What's your blue blanket going to think?"

"That's tomorrow night. We're meeting at Estel's."

"You? A date?"

"There's a whole bunch of us meeting. Tonight, I'm going solo." He jumbled a hand through stuff on my radio table. "What about a key for the door?"

"I don't lock it."

"Don't lock it?"

Down the stairs he went, patting his pockets for everything. I watched him cross over to the boards. I felt very close to him. Almost like he was my own son that I could kill one minute and kiss the next. That's probably why I had my dream about Dad again that night.

Before I went to sleep, side two had a few more songs. I mouthed the words and smoked the rest of my cigar. Nicotine is a demanding mistress.

7

The NEXT DAY, Thursday, after his first full day back on the beach, Ronny persuaded me to go with him to Estel's to meet up with Robin, two of her friends, and the rest of his crew right after work. While he showered and shaved, he filled me in on his master plan.

"The night bartender at Estel's is a good friend—at least as far as service—and the place won't be crowded at 7:00 o'clock on a weeknight. I called and arranged a little special treatment when a girl fitting Robin's description came in. This way, Highspire won't be taking care of her drinks. I told the bartender she had short, light brown hair, blue eyes, and would probably be trying to be nice to an asshole lifeguard who wouldn't let her talk."

We walked a few blocks and sat down on a bench facing the ocean because I needed a break. Ronny lit a smoke. People still on the beach packed up after being on the sand all day—umbrellas, coolers, change of clothes. Locals bundle up, some of them, clouds or no clouds, and stick it out as long as they can. I don't blame them.

Early evening is my favorite time to lounge on the beach. It's still light out, the sun sitting just above the rooftops of beachfront houses, throwing shadows to the boardwalk's edge. The arcades come alive, fluorescent lights invite pockets of kids to stand and sneak a smoke or take on a machine.

Ronny sat upright. "Shit. Here comes Peggy."

I had no idea what that woman would say about her daughter, and I didn't want to find out. Hell, I still hadn't told Ronny what went on after he left. "Where?"

"Across Ocean Ave," he pointed. Lifeguard vision. "You stick here. I'll head her off."

He crossed the street and headed in her direction. I stood up, leaned on the storm fence, and watched an osprey circling over the water. I didn't want to see what happened with those two.

The osprey dove and came up with a prize. He gave a few shakes then carried home dinner in his talons. Ronny slapped my shoulder to turn me around.

"What the fuck, Jimmy? She came right toward me; she didn't look at me. She kept glancing up waiting for the light to change. I said how's my girl. 'On the way to see your pervert friend from the other night,' she said."

I just shook my head. She had talked to Linda.

"She didn't stop. I called for her to come back, but she shot me the finger. What the hell happened after I left?"

I shrugged. Never took my voice from my pocket.

"She's fucking nuts. The first time I spent the night at her place, at three-ten—I remember the numbers on the digital clock—she sat straight up as if the house was on fire, flipped over and beat me on the chest with the fronts of her fists. Then like somebody threw a switch she looked at me with normal eyes and growled in an *Exorcist* voice, 'Did you ever get the feeling something's shit before it starts?'"

We got to Estel's and spotted Robin.

"Good evening," Ronny said. "This is my friend, Jimmy."

"I know you, Jimmy. Excuse me." Robin walked over to her two girlfriends, and then they all headed to the Gulls Room. It's Gulls and Buoys at Estel's—very Benny friendly.

"Look who's here." Ronny nodded toward Highspire, Cooper, and Vinny Fontana.

"Hoppy, you're back, man! You're fuckin' back! We need shots."

"Vinny, Jimmy."

Picture Freddie Mercury in his short hair and mustache days. Now take away the overbite and give him a Bronx accent. That's Vinny Fontana, a mix of street smarts and bullshit, which in his case might be the same thing.

Vinny and Ronny did their shots, and then Vinny latched onto two girls at the bar. He talked to them and showed them a photo from his wallet. The girls shook their heads no before turning away and laughing. Vinny came alongside of me.

"Let's see that," I pointed at his photo. He handed it to me. It was a picture of an ugly, misshapen guy.

"I tell girls it's my brother. He's lost ani'm lookin' for him. Works fifty percent of the time."

Back from the Gulls Room Robin and her friends joined the four or five guards who stood around Ronny giving him a mix of congrats and grief.

"You really back, bro?"

"On fuckin' Inlet!"

"You're back too," Ronny pointed to Robin. "Hang on. There's an open table." He cleared the empties, grabbed a bat towel, and wiped down the table. "Here we go." Robin and her friends sat. Ronny went to the bar. On the way back to the table, he found two more chairs, and we joined the girls.

The bartender brought over a bottle of champagne—Andre, not actual champagne. Either way I was shocked that Estel's even had it. We got a stack of plastic cups—no such thing as glass glasses in a beach bar just before dark.

Robin swiveled in her seat so she faced Ronny.

"I thought we'd have some bubbly to celebrate the first day of summer. I couldn't let Highspire torture you past eight."

"My God, it's that late? We should get going," Robin said.

Ronny poured. "Stay for a minute."

They twined arms and sipped. They were a very attractive couple. They both had burnished skin and straight, white teeth. Robin's eyes were bluer in the bright bar light. She had the perfect bedside manner smile—relaxed and reassuring. Her big dictionary book from the beach sat in her bag—*Stedman's Medical Dictionary*. That blue blanket from the day before folded up underneath her.

She looked at me. "Jimmy, you know you want to be careful on the beach on windy days—the blowing sand."

I smiled and made the okay sign. Our table was reunion central. All the guards stood around us.

The jukebox was between songs when Highspire started spilling the drool, talking about what sort of breasts he preferred.

Vinny laughed, "A French guy tol' me breasts should fit ina champagne glass." Highspire stared at him.

"Champagne-size cups." Ronny stood up and crushed his plastic cup against Highspire's pec. Then he opened his hand and let the fragments drop. Frankie Sinatra started crooning "My Way." Ronny said, "I love this song."

"It's the only record with a male singer ona jukebox at the lesbian bar on Cookman," Vinny said.

Robin laughed. If she saw you slip on ice and fall on your ass, her laugh wouldn't make you mad. "Come on, then," and she pulled Ronny up from his seat. They circled in one spot, people moving past them.

"Ho, that's a first," Vinny said to me. "He usually dances with barstools."

Another song came on, faster and newer— "And We Danced"—and the two of them started to whirl. They held hands with arms straight out. They spun one way and then the other, pulled each other close, and out again, all the time looking and laughing at each other, as if they'd done this a hundred times. I had a big smile on my face.

They moved to the jukebox. They each pressed some buttons. That two-out-of-three song came on—Mr. Loaf.

"No, no." Robin made a cross sign with her fingers and laughed. "No love songs in oceanside bars, Ronny." She smiled, folded her arms, and put one foot behind the other, and sang, *"Hidin' in the bottom of a Crackerjack box,"* to her beer bottle. Her two girlfriends joined in. *"I want you, I need you…"* to their beers.

Ronny stepped back. He backhanded my shoulder and pointed his chin as if to say, get this act. Robin saw his gesture and winked at me. I was a little in love with this girl.

Mr. Loaf finished. Two seconds later Ronny said to Robin, "I know a great place we can go for some quiet drinks."

I cringed.

"We have to go, remember?" Robin went to the bar and grabbed a matchbook out of a big bowl. I've seen them. They read, *We Met at Estel's 901 Ocean Ave Belmar* on the cover, and *Phone #_______________* twice on the inside. "That's practical. Room for a backup." She wrote a number on each line and handed it to Ronny.

"Champagne to toast the start of summer. Come on, you can walk us out of here." She smiled the whole time. She held out her hand to me and I took it and shook it. She had a professional's grip, assured and confident.

Ronny spit out, "Leave with me," but the three of them kept moving and Ronny ended up following them out, me right behind. I didn't want to miss this.

Outside on the porch Robin let her friends start down the stairs. "I'll be right there." She turned around, hiked her beach bag further up a shoulder, looked at Ronny and said, "It's that important to you? Impressing your friends with the old college try? Why else would you say leave with me? Like you're talking to Vinny."

She had him cold.

"My friends don't have a goddamn thing to do with it." Ronny reached for a cigarette. Robin blew out the match.

"That's not going to help anything." She put a hand on his shoulder.

He lit the cigarette anyway. "Where are you parked? All come in the same car?"

"Way down on Brystol. You stay here. We'll be just fine."

She spotted me and waved. She went down the steps to the sidewalk, one thumb under the straps of her beach bag. She looked both ways at the corner and kept herself right in the middle of the crosswalk.

"She has you pegged," I told Ronny as he passed me going back inside. He didn't say a word. Instead of going back in, I started home.

I walked the boards. The cool breeze felt better up there. Swells were kicking up. I could hear them between the cars going by. There were party boat lights on the dark horizon. All the time I've lived in Belmar, I've never seen it from the ocean at night—never been bobbing on a dot of light, having somebody on the boards wondering about me.

Summer burst out in the open. Traffic backed up. The traffic cops stood in the center of intersections, waving their white gloves and blowing their whistles.

I passed my memorial bench. There's not a plaque on it. Just the same, I bought it and then some. The summer after Sophie and I split up, I went out with some old friends, and we drank gin and who knows what else. Somebody dropped me off on Ocean Ave and took off. The rooming house where I lived sat a block or so from the beach. Standing in the street, cars passing me in bright blurs, not letting me cross, something came over me. I remember picking out, focusing on one of the boardwalk benches, and hoping up on the planks. An ocean bench—as I said, they're set in alternate directions—its back toward me. They were wooden benches, two slats across the back, stuck fence-post style into the end frames, and three slats for the seat. I circled toward the thing like a high jumper coming up on the bar, except I put both hands out in front of me and blew straight at it.

I woke up spread on what was left of the bench with my head against the wooden top rail of the storm fence. That's what stopped me and knocked me out. I started wiggling toes and fingers. I sat on the boardwalk next to the bench until I saw the red light spinning. The cops helped me up.

Next day at work, riding around on brush detail with Denny Sullivan, I pointed to the bench. Seamus, he said, how did you get your car up on the boardwalk? I had people buying me drinks all summer. It almost made up for the costs of the summons and replacing the bench.

Denny and I worked brush for years. He never married. Now with everybody thinking AIDS—even though Reagan didn't let that acronym escape his lips until a couple years ago—the summer borough workers give him heavy doses of shit from what I hear. We remained good friends after my mother walked in on us, but we were never intimate again. Who knows? Maybe that's why I married Sophie when we were both so young. I wanted to make my parents happy even though Dad had passed.

It didn't surprise me to find Peggy waiting for me when I got back to the apartment. She wasn't waiting on the boardwalk or in the downstairs foyer. She'd let herself in. I saw her face in the glow of her cigarette on the balcony.

"What kind of flapdoodle is this?"

She didn't answer, and after a second, I made for the vodka. Before the ice cubes hit glass bottom, I heard, "Nothing for me, thank you very much."

I lifted a hand and waved.

"I wouldn't want anybody taking advantage of me later on, you know? Some pervert getting me loaded and taking my clothes off. I suppose those are the only kicks you can get with a hole in your neck."

I fixed my drink. At the balcony slider, I wondered what she'd do if I closed and locked it. Probably scream and shatter the tempered glass.

I sat down with an empty chair between us. Her voice was straight razor keen. I lit a cigar, and she kept going. She repeated "I" a lot and talked in circles about *her* life. Never once did she use the words "daughter" or "Linda."

She stopped to look at me. Usually, I puff on cigars. For her I drew in some smoke through my stoma.

"Oh, my God, don't do that!"

I went inside the living room and turned on the Yankees. I turned off the sound. Peggy followed me in. She didn't stop talking. I let her go—there's Mother again. When she finally took a breath, I spit, "May I explain?"

"Explain? There's nothing to explain. There is no possible explanation. My daughter got drunk. She vomited. She lost her dress. And you saw it all."

"This is my dime. I did not touch your daughter." I kept my eyes on her. I wanted to say I have a daughter of my own. "I washed her dress. I gave her a clean sweatshirt when she woke up. Her dress is right there," I pointed to it, clean and folded on the table. "I could have called, but I didn't have your number."

"You two." Her words dragged. "Don't tell me that son of a bitch doesn't have my number. He's called me."

"Ronny wasn't here." I wanted to say I didn't have my voice. Try to fingerspell good intentions to an intoxicated, half-naked teenager. See how that works for you, loony broad. I was tired of her, tired of everybody. She didn't stay much longer—just long enough to get up the energy for a parting pop of anger.

"We'll see what Linda has to say," she spit out. She forgot to take her daughter's dress.

I don't know how many drinks and innings went by before Ronny showed up. He waved his hands in front of me. "We got trouble."

"Why are you holding your voice like that? What the hell are you saying?"

I repeated myself.

"I got no trouble. The Yanks got trouble. Second and third—the White Sox, for chrissakes. Having trouble sitting up there, buddy?"

I had one hand over the back of the couch. I don't like passing out unexpectedly, so I sit up straight all the time unless I've fixed my filter and gone to bed. The Sox got themselves a Texas leaguer.

"That's a doinker. So what's up, Jimmy? What are you talking about?"

He looked down at the table, my drink, the vodka bottle, the ashtray. He picked up a cigarette filter. "These butts from tonight? Peggy smokes Kools."

"A loud woman let herself into my home."

"She was here, huh? Cigars, too. You guys have a party?" He paced. After a few steps, "So what's going on?"

"Last night, after your dramatic exit, Linda stayed around for a while. She threw up—"

"I saw that, for chrissakes."

"She threw up on her dress after I helped her up. It was stupid. I didn't like seeing that mess on her dress."

"Here," he brought me a glass of water. "So what happened? Put the cigar in the ashtray, will you? You're going to burn the place down."

"She was out of it, and I took her dress off, to rinse in the tub. I did that and hung it on the railing to dry."

"Where was she? Where the hell was *she?*"

"The spare room."

"*My* room. She wakes up without her dress in my room and runs home to mom. Oh, that's fuckin' groovy, Jimmy. Shit! Did she run home topless?" He bent down and got right in my face.

I didn't look at him. I shook my head. "I didn't touch her and I'm damn tired of repeating myself." If everybody had to speak the way I do, there'd be fewer stupid statements hanging out over the ocean waiting to drop and sink into oblivion.

"I put my big Belmar Subs sweatshirt on her."

He got himself a drink. "Ah, horseshit. Work tomorrow, all this today, and last night. She wasn't wearing a bra, for chrissakes. Tell me what Peggy said tonight." He lit a cigarette and started to laugh. "Wait, before you tell me that, tell me *exactly* what happened last night after Linda woke up."

"I couldn't talk to her. Couldn't tell her what was going on." I held up my voice and pointed to it. "Remember? I couldn't tell her what I wanted to do for her."

"What did she say?"

"'Where's my dress? This is no dress.'"

"And she ran out? With you waving your hands around, I bet, trying to fingerspell to her. So what did Peggy say?"

I waved a hand at him and changed channels. Donald O'Conner in *Singin' in the Rain* popped on.

"She couldn't have been that upset if you explained things to her."

O'Conner was on the couch with that dummy. I love it when he flips off the walls. I poured two shots of vodka. "Sure. Cheers."

He watched the TV. He sat down and took a few sips before asking, "What the hell can she do? What do you think she'll do?"

"Watch the movie." I got up and went out to the balcony. Horns were honking; people were calling to each other—almost the weekend. All that talking, the walking to and from Estel's, waiting up for Ronny to give him the news.

Next thing I heard, "Let's go, Jimmy." I dozed on the balcony. Ronny helped me up. "Gotta work tomorrow, sleep now." He was calmed and sleepy. He's lucky like that—things bother him about five minutes, then they're history.

"Go on. One more scene." He had the TV off, and I turned it back on— *with* volume. I switched on the AC and closed the balcony. I also locked the door. That woman was dangerous—I hadn't decided yet about her daughter.

I had no idea what Linda had told her mother, but I wasn't about to tell Ronny the truth—that Linda never did pass out or fall asleep. She splashed her face with cold water when I came in from watching Ronny walk away. She saw the puke on her dress and asked me if I had something for her to wear. She peeled off the dress as if we were in the girl's locker room. I turned right around, pulled the door shut, and got her my oversized sweatshirt. I opened the door a few inches and poked it into her. When she came out, she asked where Ronny went, and when I told her he walked south behind the dance bar, she took off to catch up to him.

I thought about Linda and Peggy until Gene's big scene came on. The sun's in my heart, and I'm ready for love. The more I watched Gene dancing, splashing that cop at the end, the more I smiled. I hadn't had many spontaneous smiles lately. Ronny's first weekend back on the beach, all the excitement of the past two days… It was summer—Ronny had even toasted it. Anything could happen.

8

FRIDAY BROKE GRAY and uncertain—the kind of day a mother isn't sure how to dress her children before they go off to school. I moved between coffee at J's and sessions under Annie's umbrella. Around ten, it started to drizzle.

Guards don't leave because of rain—only thunder. Ronny had to stick around with Harris and Cooper. Those two drew most of the stand time—Harris because he was a rookie and Cooper because he loves to sit up there. Ronny tipped the guard boat and propped it on the oars so the gunnel kept the rain off him.

I squatted under Annie's umbrella as I watched a heavy shower move east like a curtain, first across Ocean Ave, then the boards and the sand, then droplets out over the water, past the barrels and beyond. It washed all the morning beachgoers home.

Highspire finally sent Ronny home around three. He'd told me he planned to lie low for a while—at least for the weekend—and that he'd decided to take a room at the Commodore. He didn't want to stick around here because of Peggy, and I couldn't blame him.

I hadn't slept the night before either. Annie talked about age spots. When she started to make sense to me, I headed home for a nap of my own.

Around eight o'clock I got a phone call from Ronnie.

"Come over and have a cocktail with me. They have munchie food—chicken wings or something."

"That's an eight block walk home in the dark for me."

"We just had the longest day in the year."

"No booze tonight." I hate talking on the phone. It's two hands full of too much. My radio has a standing mike. That I don't mind.

"Room 232 if I'm not in the lounge."

"The lounge. What is this lounge called? The Piss Palace?"

"All right, all right. It happens to be the Engine Room."

I knew the Commodore. I lived there a month one summer a long time ago, and aside from generations of vermin, it probably hadn't changed much. The hallways and rooms were the same color—nicotine gray. The doors were black, the woodwork and molding were black, too. The only lights in the hallways that worked were the red exit lights at either end—the others would get stolen by guests to replace burned out bulbs in their rooms. It was possible to sit in a bathroom stall for minutes and never sense somebody nearby until he flushed. Places like the Commodore are rare nowadays. The beachside property is worth ten times the physical structure. *Raze* is the realtor's favorite verb after *sell*.

The Commodore's outside looked the same, but when I went in the lobby—man, they jazzed the place up. The walls were bright, the black trim and doors were all light, natural wood, and the hard wood floors had been refinished. Inside the lounge sat a new bar, its outer edge inlaid with three-strand manila line, like a dock or seaside pier. On the walls were old photos of the town, of fishing boats, record fish caught along with the statistics—that sort of thing. The bar's equipment was all new. Clean, shiny appointments, chrome tap heads.

Then I went upstairs. Well, just the first floor. Still the dungeon décor from what I could tell by the hall. I peeked into a vacant room. Sure enough, downstairs is where the new owner threw his money. Liquor rings the register; it also makes the rooms tolerable.

I watched people shuffle into the lobby and find their way to the bar. It was Friday, after all. There were local guys, a lot of them fresh from their jobs, not home to the wife just yet, looking for a little distraction to get the weekend going. Of course the Bennys and the Bennys carrying bags and duffels, talking way too loud because, after all, they were here for their fun. Their money paid the locals' bills in winter. They didn't care about anything other than the dreadnought called the weekend.

Each beachside establishment has its own personality and type of crowd it caters to. The owner dictates décor; customers decide atmosphere. The Commodore tried Monday night turtle races a few summers back. The regulars hated it because the Bennys liked it. Some of the regulars quit coming. As a regular, I figured I couldn't get rid of the Bennys, so I got rid of one or two turtles at a time. I found good homes for them.

I sat at the bar. They had Bud on tap. Ronny came down from his room on the second floor, and we ordered two beers.

The Engine Room had a pool table—an old, slate-top number with fancy leather webbing for pockets. A couple shot 8-ball—he a Civil War-bearded, Sixties holdover wearing a ball cap, jeans, and T-shirt, she a short, heavy set smile machine dressed in red-light bright matching pullover and slacks. The guy walked around the table as if looking into a potluck stew and the woman— she just couldn't wipe that grin off her plain, round face. They were playing eight ball. All his stripes were gone, and all of her solids were sitting, and for a good ten shots, no words passed her teeth or the beer foam sitting on his mouth-covering mustache. Then he slammed the eight ball, trying to sink it even though all those solids had the table clogged. The cue ball headed straight for the corner pocket where she stood. She reached down, caught the ball before it fell, and swirled it in her palm. Then she took it down to the other end, spotted right on the dot and lined up another miss.

Ronny and I sat around. We watched the pool couple play another game—same story. The guy just couldn't bring himself to sink the eight. We were on draft #2 when Ronny pointed, "Oh boy. Nelson."

"Nelson?"

"Something Nelson. I went to elementary school with him. Played ball with him, then against him in high school. He's the kind of jerk who lets you into his club as long as you keep on paying dues. Last thing I heard was he— you see that? He looked right at me and then kept looking around."

A commuter—the guy looked like he just jumped off the train from the city. Ronny stood up and raised his hand.

"Nellie!" he yelled. "Nel-lie! Nel-lie!" He chanted it like the crowds at Yankee Stadium used to chant Reg-gie, Reg-gie. Nellie brought a hand up to his shoulder, showed a washed palm, and then came over. Short and stocky, with a nice little pot belly, a beautiful suit, tie still tight against the collar, gold cufflinks, the Rolex, the whole bit. He and Ronny shook hands. Judging from the shake's duration and their forearms shaking, they must have squeezed for all they were worth.

Nellie smirked, "Don't have a hot date at Bar Bombay?" Bar Bombay is one of those fern bars—big ferns hanging all over. Places like that keep making comebacks, and I don't know why.

"So, Rescue Ronny, are you paying by the drink or the hour these days?" Nellie explained to me, "We called him Rescue Ronny after he shit himself in first grade. The teacher had to rescue him from the boy's room."

"Rescue Ronny. What's your pleasure, Nellie?"

Nellie ordered a Dewar's on the rocks.

Ronny peeled off a twenty from his roll. Another twenty twirled under that, and so on. I've seen his cash rolls. Nothing smaller than tens. He carries either cash or sponges off somebody— with him, you never know.

"This is different." Nellie ran a hand along the rope on the bar top's edge.

"We do big things in this town."

"Yeah, right," Nellie smiled. "So you still the lifelong lifeguard?"

Ronny didn't skip a beat. "Just started today."

"This guy your date?" Nellie laughed. He pointed to my neck with his Dewar's. "He let you stick it in his throat?"

"Oh, yeah," Ronny put down his beer and stepped away from the bar. "Remember that time you drove the baseline that second game our senior year? When we were home? I swatted your little floater into the climbing ropes. What did I say? That shit don't flush. Remember?"

Nellie didn't say anything.

"Yeah, I put that bullshit *away*, just like *that!*" When Ronny said *that*, he snapped his fingers on his left hand inches from Nellie's eyes and brought up a right that smacked Nellie's glass hard just as he sipped his drink. The glass broke and then fell, and Nellie put both hands up to his mouth, blood running between his fingers, turned around and disappeared out the door.

I took a sip of beer. "Amazing. Which comment did it?"

"You know me. One comment after another. Plus it's this business with Peggy. It really pisses me off, her walking right into your place. As a matter of fact, I'm thinking about heading over there tonight."

I put my hand on his arm and shook my head.

He ignored me. He finished his beer, picked up the bigger pieces of Nelson's glass and put them along with a ten on the bar, winked at the bartender and turned to leave.

"Hang on." I caught up to him. "It doesn't pay to stick around after altercations. People go on friend searches and show up looking for payback. Nowadays the only friend they need is in their glove compartment."

"Translation—you're coming to Peggy's with me. Okay, daddy. Let's go."

Up and down Monmouth, back up lights turned to parallel park. In an hour, there'd be a premium on every foot of curb space. Ocean Ave looked slick and black from the mist.

We were in the crosswalk on Chester—Peggy's street, it turned out—just when this car pulled a surprise right turn. It damn near hit us.

We should have taken it as a sign even though I don't believe in them.

Peggy's house was three blocks from the ocean. There were lights on downstairs—it was just twilight. I touched Ronny's arm. "Don't do anything stupid."

"I'm going to play dumb—make believe I don't know anything about her visit with you."

I made myself at home on the front steps of a rooming house across the street. Ronny tried the screen door, but it was locked. He rang the bell.

Peggy opened the front door, saw him, took hold of the door's edge, and slammed it in his face. He stood there on the porch for a minute, then put his thumb on the doorbell and held it in. I could hear shouting through the upstairs screens even across the street. It was Linda and Peggy. Ronny switched thumbs on the bell—I couldn't hear it ring for all the yelling.

Then Linda called through a screen, "Get out of here. She's calling the cops!"

"Let her!" Ronny lit a cigarette, walked down to the curb in front of the house and sat down.

I stood up and walked across the street. "What the hell are you doing? Let's go."

"If she wants to act like an asshole, I'll give her a mark to shoot for."

A minute later, a cruiser pulled up and stopped. Peggy and Linda were still going at it. I knew one of the cops—Paulie Dalton. So did Ronny.

"You hear the yelling going on in there officer Dalton?"

"What do you know about it, Hopkins?"

He shrugged and flicked his cigarette into the street. "I was just leaving." Dalton looked at Ronny, at me, and then at the house.

"Let's go," Dalton said to his partner. They both got out of the cruiser and started up the walk.

I grabbed Ronny's arm. "Let's get the hell out of here."

"Not yet." Ronny waited for a finger to hit the bell. The second it did, he yelled "Peggy!" The cops turned and looked at us. "Okay, now we can go." Five houses down he called back, "She's a maniac!"

At the boardwalk, he picked up the receiver of a goddamn pay phone.

"I can't resist." The next time he talked, he disguised his voice. "How's your bell? Your bell! How's your stinkin' doorbell?" He tried not to laugh. Then his face went blank, and he hung up.

"Who did you get?"

"Oh, I got Peggy, all right."

"What did she say?"

"She didn't talk into the receiver. I heard something like it's him…the phone…rape. That last word shot up my back."

"Get away from me. Go to the Commodore. I'm going home."

These two were playing paddleball with each other, the kind with the rubber string stapled to the little wooden paddle, banging out, jerking back. Ronny headed north; I headed south—six blocks to his two.

At home, I figured my night was over. Wrong. Two phone calls kept me awake—the first from officer Bauer of the Belmar PD. When you've lived your life in a town that has one elementary school, 6,000 people nine months a year, then 25,000 for three months, those 6,000 get to know a lot of each other. Officer Bauer knew us both, and of course so did Dalton from the cruiser at Peggy's.

After I hung up with Bauer, I relaxed on the couch, no shirt. I had a bottle of Smirnoff's hundred proof nestled between my legs. I sipped it and watched TV until Ronny placed call number two.

"Greetings from the Engine Room. Hey, I'm sorry about that Peggy shit."

I held out the receiver. "Not to mention the Engine Room assault and battery plus one other interesting event."

"What was the interesting event?"

"Our policeman friend officer Bauer already called."

"You're kidding. Why'd he call you? What did Bowser say?"

"Because you have no known address or phone number. He said he didn't want to call your mother and worry her. Peggy put out a complaint. Bauer didn't go into specifics. It might be just about ringing her bell. I don't know." I stopped on the edge of telling him what a stupid bastard he was because I realized I hadn't been so smart myself.

"What's with her yelling rape?"

I started to laugh. The phlegm came up and I cleared my filter.

"It's not funny, goddamn it. But it's getting there. I could be fined. Fined by the same borough that pays my salary. Will the irony of this night never cease?"

"Stop." We were both laughing. It took me a minute to stop. "You could get your ass thrown in jail, and then get an advance on your salary to post bail."

"Ah, I still don't like the R word."

"It's your ass she wants—your bankroll. Is it surprising, Mr. Money Bags? Nobody raped anybody. Who did she mean, Linda? You weren't even here. You left, remember?"

"So she's just trumping this up?"

"Sure. Bauer's going to talk to you himself. He remembers—"

"My father. Yeah, yeah, yeah."

"Small town charm."

"He's coming to the Commodore?"

"The beach," I smiled. "Officer Bauer—I wouldn't call him Bowser if I were you—is coming right down to your guard stand tomorrow. A Saturday showcase."

He didn't say anything for a few seconds. "I'll stay here for the night. Three days ago, I wouldn't have cared. Now I have the job to lose. And that nurse. I like that nurse."

"Spare me."

"Hey, some guy—he saw us in here before—he called you Shameless Seamus. He said how'd you meet Shameless Seamus. I would've kicked his ass for you, but I'm all used up."

9

THERE'S AN IRISH song called "Jug of Punch." One verse says, "And if I get drunk, well the money's me own. And them don't like me they can leave me alone." I think of that song when somebody calls me by that old nickname—Shameless Seamus.

It's been twenty-five years. The facts should be hazy. They're not.

Around dusk, I left our house. My wife Sophie and I rented a small place on Barclay. I headed on my bike over the Inlet Bridge to my friend Ed's place four blocks down from the beach in Avon. Sophie stayed home to watch Alice. Around two, she walked and talked. Sophie had been out the night before with her girlfriends. Now it was my turn.

There were supposed to be a few guys having some beers on a Saturday night. Ed had a tiny house tucked between two bigger places about a block down from the Avon Inn. I saw him out on the slat porch sitting in a beach chair when I rode up his walk. A Coasters record played inside. Ed twisted a can of Bud out of a six-pack and flipped it to me. He handed me a can opener.

I opened the beer. "Where is everybody on this fine summer Saturday?"

"Got me." Not much for words and my age, Ed worked odd jobs at the time. Short and slight, a step behind most people, he kept to himself, minded his own business. He looked like a gopher—always squinting behind his long nose.

It was obvious Ed had the makings of a serious drinking problem even then. I should talk. Back then, I stuck to beer. Ed always had a pint bottle of cheap brandy along with his six-pack. He'd nip at first, but then halfway down the bottle he'd take good, long pulls. He used to hold out the bottle and offer it to me. I'd politely refuse. The more he drank, the more he would hang that bottle in front of my face until finally, after I said no, thank you, for the tenth time, he would say, "Well then fuck you, Hanlon. I suppose my whiskey's not good enough."

Still on his first sip offer, things were pleasant.

"What a peaceful, pleasant view watching the quiet cars go past under the streetlights." I loved alliteration.

"The horseshit that comes out of your mouth," Ed laughed. I laughed with him. We talked about work and women. I was free and clear for the night.

A few guys showed up. They each talked about Billy Carney having a party over on Locust. A keg and lots of girls.

"Oh, yeah?" Ed wasn't going anyplace with two sixes and his brandy. He was anchored fast to his place.

Monkey Flannigan stopped by. "Come on over, Seamus," his car running, double-parked in front of Ed's.

The idea appealed to me. Crowds were my element. I looked at Ed's expression before he lifted his brandy for a slug. His mouth curled down at a corner just before he put his lips around the bottleneck.

"I'll hang here," I told Monkey.

Ed perked up after Monkey left. He dug into his records and came out with some real gems. He put on Chuck Berry. He put on my request—the Four Tops. We smoked cigarettes and drank while the stars came out over the treetops. We lit candles and stuck them in Mateus wine bottles.

Around nine-thirty—I wore a watch in those days—two girls walked past the house. They were talking loudly, laughing. They disappeared down the street, and I didn't think anything of it. Five minutes later, they were back, a little louder than the first go-round.

"Watch this," Ed hit my arm. "Hey, who goes there?"

"The Supremes," one girl laughed. They stopped at the end of Ed's walk, giggling and whispering.

"The Supremes, huh? Diana Ross with you?"

The girls came closer. When they were in sight, I thought they looked about seventeen, maybe eighteen. One wore a white top with puffy sleeves.

"You guys share beer?"

Ed laughed and handed the girl one beer. They didn't bat an eye. They shared it back and forth and emptied it.

"We'll be back," white top giggled down the walk.

"We'll be here. Like hell you will," Ed snickered after they were gone.

Again, a few beers passed, and I didn't think twice about those girls. Ed put on the Everly Brothers. "Girls love the Brothers."

"Did you know those two?"

"Hell, no."

"All I Have to Do Is Dream" started when the girls came up Ed's walk. "Here they are." This time he peeled off two beers for them. White top opened hers and sat right down on my lap just as easy as you please.

"We took some pills," she whispered in my ear. I didn't know what to do. The other girl, who was heavy set and big up top, had her arms around Ed's neck. She leaned over and whispered something to him I couldn't hear.

Ed picked up his brandy and both walked into the tiny cottage—one couch and one big chair in the living room, Ed's bedroom and the bathroom. The bathroom didn't even have a door. Ed had nailed a shower curtain onto the top molding.

I heard voices in the living room. Then Ed's bedroom door closed.

White top rolled off my lap and made for the cottage. I followed her. She went into the living room and flopped on the couch. She put an arm under her head.

"I am so sleepy. I think I'm going to pass out."

Don and Phil crooned away. I stepped outside. One of the candles burned crooked. Red wax ran down the bottle's side onto the spool table, the flame batting side to side. I peeked inside. The girl hadn't budged. Her top lifted off her bare waist. One ankle lay over the other, and a flip-flop rested on the floor.

I went in and sat down on the couch's edge. I had to squish her one leg over. I rubbed her back with my palm, her lower back where her blouse lifted. Her skin was warm. I held a beer in one hand and touched under her blouse with the other. I touched the small of her back and her hip. That's all I touched.

I heard things outside—a car going by, somebody calling. I didn't hear anything coming from Ed's bedroom. Then the last song on the record ended. The tone arm slid across the wide grooves at the label, lifted with a pop, then swung back over its armrest before it dropped, and the turntable clicked off.

I'm not claiming to be some kind of moral compass. I never should have sat on that couch alongside an unconscious girl. As a father—and yes, I was a father that night—I can say I'd beat anyone who touched my daughter under those circumstances.

White top wasn't passed out. Curiosity, I suppose, on her part. What it felt like to be touched. Now I know teenage girls sometimes do that.

She and her friend weren't seventeen. They weren't even fifteen. They were thirteen years old. They were seventh graders. Whatever went on in Ed's bedroom—I never found out—it sure as hell must have been more involved than what happened in the living room.

The heavy-set girl came banging out Ed's bedroom door screaming at the top of her lungs—so loud that White Top shot up like all the couch springs decided to launch her.

Next day at work one Avon and one Belmar cop showed up. They pointed to me, and away we went to the station. Corruption of minors the legal wording went. I gave beer to an underage girl. It may as well have been a much more inflammatory phrase—take your pick. That's what went around Belmar, and that's what stuck.

It was Ed's house and Ed's beer—even though it turned out the girls had had quite a few of their own beers. White top—she never told me her name, and to protect a minor I never learned it. She told her parents and the authorities that nothing occurred of a sexual nature. I didn't go to trial and get convicted like Ed. No matter.

My life became a trash pile of inferred details. Sophie and I were never the same. We only lasted a few more months. *Your incident* she called it. It always came up. Maybe I lived down to her expectations. We were always one word away from some kind of sharp edge. She wasn't alone in not forgetting. Sometimes a whole town remembers, including my son-in-law.

10

THE WEEKEND—AND I was on the beach early. The morning haze drifted out over the water with the offshore breeze as the walkers and runners logged their boardwalk time. I settled under my umbrella and looked around for people. Bauer, Peggy, Robin—maybe Peggy with a formal complaint in one hand and a gun in the other.

Cooper showed up first. He locked his bike to the storm fence and started his ritual. First, he folded his windbreaker and tucked it into his knapsack. Out of the storage locker came sweatshirt, sweatpants and cap, all faded red, last year's official borough issue, with BELMAR GUARD in white block letters across the chest, down the right leg, and across the bill. Then the sand chair for his wife, Denise, who usually came late morning to bring him a nice, fresh-made sandwich. She would sit in her usual spot just outside the Benny rope. Cooper would sit on the same side of the stand where Denise sat. All the guards had to do to drive Cooper to mumble obscenities would be to wait until he left the stand for some reason and then slide over to Denise's end.

The Benny rope only extended around the sides and back of the stand. The guards had to keep the front of the stand open. It's amazing how many people on crowded days tried to camp out right in front of the stand, right next to the torps sticking in the sand so they could be snatched for a save. Most of the locals know better. Guess the Bennys figure that since they paid for their beach badge and drove down from the city all that way, they can sit wherever the hell they want. The guards would say do you want to block our way if it's your kid who's crying out. And it's the mothers with their new hairdos and make-up—on the *beach*, for chrissakes—who give the guards the most trouble.

After he had all his clothing in his arms, Cooper dug into his knapsack for his Panama Jack bag—a clear plastic bag with every Panama Jack suntan product known to white people. Sun or no sun, he'll put that on top of his laundry and stack everything in the space Annie's trying to set up. He usually managed to put it right on top of her cross-stitch.

61

I have never seen Cooper contribute to the morning set-up. The boat and stand must be unlocked from the dead man—that's a log buried deep as a security anchor. Drag down the stand and dig it in. Run the boat down close to the shoreline. Set the oars. Check the lines. Set-up is also when Vinny gives his rundown on who, where and what from the previous night.

After the guards finished set-up, they had morning workouts. The workouts are laps between the barrel lines, sometimes a run to the Inlet Ave jetty and then a swim back, and of course, a hard-core swim to the jetty and back. Many Jersey beaches still use swim areas bordered on north and south by thick ropes. The ropes attach to an anchor on the ocean bottom and a dead man buried up the beach. Barrels keep the lines afloat. The last barrel is an old beer keg with a chain connecting it to the heavy iron V-anchor that grabs the bottom.

Vinny and Ronny took the first shift on the stand. There were some early birds down but nobody in the water except Harris and Cooper swimming barrels. Highspire stood in front of the stand with his hands on his hips. He turned and smiled up.

"You two next." He walked down by the water.

"Everything I heard's true," Vinny said.

"No," Ronny replied, "he's a much bigger asshole than you've heard." He tilted his head up. "Got to get that morning sun on my face."

"You cold? Takya shirt off."

"It's early. We'll all get enough sun today."

Vinny turned on Harris's radio. "I give the antenna a week. Ten bucks."

"You'll break it on day six."

"Look, Coopa quit," Vinny, pointed. Cooper waded in.

Vinny hit Ronny's arm, and they were off the stand, sprinting on either side of Highspire for the water. They were free and clear of the breakers in no time, swimming for the bright orange, north keg barrel bobbing with each wave. They got out there and started across the area for the south barrel. Harris had just come off that one—they swam ten laps. Vinny and Ronny took their time, but Harris busted ass, elbows high, arms cutting the surface like pocketknives coming open.

Then he started veering out. Guards are in the habit of looking up, keeping the victim in sight. Billy Harris the rookie headed for my ancestral home in Ireland.

Vinny got to the south barrel first, sat on the line, and cupped his hands, calling Harris. Right after Ronny got there, he quit yelling. They both sat on the line, the barrel dipping under with their weight. Harris swam as if something was after him.

All this time Highspire blew the hell out of his Acme Thunderer, trying to get Harris to look up. Finally, he did, and he corrected to dead north.

Ronny and Vinny finished their laps, came in, and dried off near the stand. Harris swam until he closed in on the jetty. Then he turned south.

"Harris is swimming the jetty." Cooper pointed.

"I see him," Ronny said. "He's breast stroking now. He's a hell of a swimmer, except he doesn't look where he's going. Now he's back to his crawl. He keeps a nice, constant stroke. Good reach, steady kick. His head's too low in the water so he turns way around for a breath. See how it pulls him strong to one side? Then he has to compensate with his breaststroke."

"What's the tide doing?" a lady asked Cooper. She held down a straw hat with both hands. I felt a breath of breeze.

"Ronny knows."

"Ma'am?"

"What's the tide doing?"

"Would you like it to change or keep still?"

"Keep still. We don't want to put our blanket where the waves will get it. We're here with our grandsons."

"Right now the water's deciding which way it wants to go." Ronny walked the woman to a spot above the tide line. Het set up her umbrella, came back, lit a smoke, and settled on the stand. "Rumor has it the new guard gear's coming today."

The last bit of business before the crowds came—a line job. Highspire picked Cooper to swim out and be the victim for Ronny. Some beaches don't practice the line saving rescue any longer. They prefer a surfboard rescue, or just a guard with a torp. In rough water, it's always nice to have that yellow coil of line in the bucket. A lot can go wrong—the line can tangle, the guard's belt can slip down below the waist—but if four or five people are in the same run, a lot can go right. Inlet Ave had some nasty runs. They needed a line.

Cooper was a hundred feet or so past the last barrel, and Ronny took off, outside the swimming area because there were a few bathers. He made it out there just fine, got a hold of Cooper, and Highspire and Vinny worked the line. What pluck! They took turns taking the line up the beach, then turning and running back to the water's edge, always keeping the line taught with a good, steady pull. Everybody was pleased.

The rest of the morning flew by. No Bauer, Peggy, or Robin. Matter of fact I didn't see many people I recognized, but that didn't surprise me. Inlet never was my beach.

A good crowd gathered. A lot of couples and groups but not many families with kids running all over the place. No gay stuff either. Par for the beach. Belmar has a raft beach and a surfing beach. Those are facts. Some say it has family beaches and teen beaches, gay beaches, and drug beaches, local, Benny, and black beaches. Those are all rumors or word of mouth—from week to week sometimes. What it's always got are wide, clean, sandy beaches. That's why it won't ever die.

Cooper took first lunch. Vinny and Ronny sat up top. Highspire dug in behind the stand doing crunches. He sincerely believed it got him women, and he took his time. He dug two holes, put his legs in up to his knees, and went to town. He counted aloud and cheated. When he hissed a number, he let go of his air as he relaxed at the top of his exercise. If he grunted it, he stopped halfway up and threw his arms forward.

"What's your record, Highspire?"

"About six hundred. One-seventy," he grunted.

"Six hundred my ass," I laughed.

"Niblet at three o'clock," Vinny said. Niblet was guard slang for any young girl after the sweet corn by the same name. Vinny's Niblet walked north in a V-cut two-piece. "Some job. I want her to have my children."

"Niblets," Ronny said. "It's no wonder. TV, movies, everyday magazines. They all scream the same thing. What the hell. Women have younger men."

The girl walked back the other way.

"That's a nice feecha on 'his beach. If they walk goin' north, they gotta come back south."

Highspire's noises bothered me. I walked around to the front of the stand. Harris sat on the lower step with his nose in some book. I pointed at the book.

"What is that?"

"You say something?" he looked up. "Whoa."

My stoma felt his stare.

"This is Jimmy," Ronny climbed down. "Jimmy's a pal, a guard's best friend."

"What happened to him?"

"Try asking him."

"What happened to you?"

"I lost my larynx in the sand." The kid stared down.

"Harris, answer the man's question. What book is that? You know you can't take that upstairs, right? No reading on the stand."

"Yeah." Harris was still flustered. "It's a summer course. Sociology."

"A summa korse?" Vinny said.

Ronny took the book. "Growth Periods of Adulthood. We havta takea closa look at dis korse, Vinny."

"He's makin' funna me, Jimmy."

"I know how you feel."

"Here's a big colored chart. Let's see what the authors have to say about people like Highspire. How about Cooper? Research on Vinny is probably being double-checked. See this, Jimmy?" He showed me with a finger. "Early Adult Transitional Stage includes eighteen-year-olds. That's you, Harris. Vinny, they got you in here after all. At twenty-three, you're in the Entering Stage. I'm stuck in Age Thirty Transition."

"No," I pointed, "you're thirty-three, the earliest year of Settling Down Period. Harris' book took your excuse."

"Settling Down goes to thirty-*five*. I have two more years. You're my witness, Vinny."

Vinny looked down at the book with a blank expression. "You havta make the transition, Hoppy. See where it says Transition all the way across? You can't go on like this. Peggy, Bauer, Casivette. I'm telling you, you're in a transition. Tell Peggy that. You're atta crossroads."

Ronny looked up at Vinny. "That's a terrific plan."

"Ah, restroom break, highness," Vinny said back to Highspire, who had switched to his morning Tai Chi. Harris and Ronny climbed up. Harris grabbed his radio to change channels. Always with him, it's a blur of sounds, a song for a few seconds, then another until the perfect tune. Up goes the volume, out come the imaginary drumsticks and he's off to the concert.

Ronny's turn came. He dialed CBS 101.1—oldies. Harris made a major production out of having to listen to a doo-wop song. Ronny handed it back, and Harris started his routine again.

"That's a tuner, Harris, not a padlock."

"Maybe you're approaching that Settling Down Period faster than you thought," I said.

The lunch turns moved along, and the afternoon settled in like a kid next to his sandcastle. The sun hit me hard and hot, so I camped under my umbrella for the duration. It was quiet time. A lot of people go home between three and four headed for bars or big Saturday night plans. The swimmers are mostly kids whose parents stick around. The kids stay in until they're wrinkled and blue.

A mother screamed and threatened one of them.

"The kid begged, "Five more minutes."

Three, four more times before the mother went into her act. She stood up and called, "We're going right *now*! We're leaving this minute!"

The father took his nose from behind the *Daily News*. "Goddamn it, Peter, Jr.! Get up here!"

"Language!"

Peter, Jr. was still catching waves—or trying to. He was a roly-poly, and not a strong swimmer. He dropped off the peak every time.

A southeast breeze picked up. It got a little chilly, but that's June. I saw Casivette coming down from Annie's gate. I went to the stand, hit Ronny's foot and pointed back with a thumb before retreating under my umbrella.

Ronny fired up a smoke watching Casivette come down the beach. "Look at him. Like he's in his backyard, and the people are his roses."

Casivette stood in front of the stand. "That helps your wind, Hopkins."

"Looking for Highspire? He's at lunch."

"Nope, just you." Casivette took a folded, yellow piece of loose-leaf paper from his jacket pocket and held it out. It fluttered in the breeze. "Read it."

"An employee of the borough under your direction..." Ronny read, "...annoyance complaint against said woman and her daughter...employee shall refrain from further behavior which could cause severe mental anguish...blah, blah. Thanks, Casivette. You're very efficient. So are you going to fire me a week early instead of after the Fourth?"

"You read it. I don't want it—that's your copy. I'm just here to relay the message. The chain of command."

"The layers of bird seed. I get it. Sure thing. Tell whomever that this employee told the crazy woman good-bye." Casivette did a right face and left. Ronny smiled at me when I came to the stand.

"That bull about Bauer coming down here was just that, Jimmy."

"Was whomever correct?"

"I thought it sounded fancy. Look who's here."

"The one?" I looked, and then I saw her. "Casivette intercepted her. A fate worse than sobriety."

"You're a little unsteady, Jimmy. Been at your thermos, eh? C'mon Robin. Walk away from that asshole."

I shifted my feet and hung onto the stand. I wanted to watch this great reunion after twenty-four hours had passed. I wanted to see Ronny fall on his face to be honest. Maybe I was jealous. He was on one hell of a winning streak, and he didn't appreciate it one bit.

"Oh, she'll be down. You're here."

"Jesus, Jimmy. You look like Cagney in *Yankee Doodle Dandy*. Have a seat." He put me on the lower step of the stand. "Be a lifeguard," he gave me a little salute.

"I had a speech all set for Bauer."

"I'd say we worried about nothing."

"No live witnesses. You get bored if you don't have something to bitch about. You're not happy unless somebody else is pissed."

"Yeah, yeah. There he goes. Now she's talking to Denise."

"Who?"

"Denise, Cooper's wife. She sat way up the beach today..."

With that, Ronny was up the beach. He spoke to Robin for a minute before they walked through Annie's gate and south down the boardwalk.

I needed some home recovery. I got some cold seltzer from Vinny before I packed everything up. For some reason—probably because of the seltzer—I invited Harris and Vinny back to my apartment for drinks at dusk. What a mistake.

At eleven-thirty, my whole apartment pulsed with light and sound. Dion and The Belmonts harmonized all the way to the corner. *Don't know why I love you don't know why I care...* Vinny tried to sing. His Bronx came through loud and clear. He started flicking the light switch on and off to the bass man's background vocal, but his rhythm was way off. That record was shot— scratches galore.

Ronny came up the steps.

I turned down the volume. Vinny kept right on with the lights. Harris sat on the floor against the couch, a big smile on his face, his arms spread flat on the cushions.

Ronny pointed at Harris. "A happy crucifixion. It's the police!"

Harris sat up like a shot. After a minute of hugs, I held up a palm.

"What gives?"

"What gives with you?" Ronny said. "Sit down and catch your breath. What's with Harris?"

"Rites of passage. He's flunking."

"Jimmy, turn it up, man," Vinny said. I obliged and motioned for Ronny to follow me into the bathroom.

"Those two. I had a nap and made dinner, but Vinny discovered the liquor cabinet. The rest is out there before your eyes. So what gives?"

He sat on the toilet and lit a cigarette. "You wouldn't believe me if I told you."

"Are you tired? You want a drink?"

"I don't want a drink. I just want to get some sleep. The Commodore is a little loud. At least I thought it was loud before I got here."

"You look like hell."

"You should smell my shorts."

"What the hell are you talking about?"

"Tomorrow, Jimmy. I'll tell you all about it tomorrow."

He stood to leave, but I blocked his way with my arm. "Have a cocktail. It's going to rain tomorrow."

"You're way ahead of me."

"No, I've had water since the beach. I'll kick Laurel and Hardy out, and we'll have a cocktail. You'll tell me about your night."

"Okay, Jimmy, okay."

We went out, but Ronny did a quick about face and went back into the bathroom. The shower came on. In the living room, Harris had climbed onto the couch. He had a silly expression on his face as if he wanted to smile but all the air had gone out of his cheeks. Vinny primped in the mirror. His night stretched ahead to the horizon. He spoke to his reflection.

"Forget Hoppy. When he hits the showers, it's lights out."

He pinched my ear, and the two of us helped Harris down the steps. Back upstairs I made Ronny and me cocktails—very light—and we sat down on the couch after he came out from his shower. He thought a second, and then he started.

11

H E WENT BACK to the last time I saw him when he walked up the beach after Casivette finally left. He said he was going for a restroom break, but it was to talk to Robin. In passing, he asked her to take a walk. He kept going in case Casivette turned around. They met at Annie's gate and walked the block toward the restrooms. Small talk—weather, where her friends were. Then she said, "You lost my matches. You didn't call. Did you lose my number?"

He launched into an epic and stopped short just before his nose got too long. "Between moving to the Commodore and the new job…half my shit's there, half of it's here—"

Robin must have been in a forgiving mood, because the next thing he knew, she told him, "I'll meet you at the Commodore at eight."

He watched her walk back to Annie. It was the first time he'd seen her from behind in a bathing suit. She filled it just right. Mitch Rider—not too skinny, not too fat. That's what he thought about for the next two hours—seeing Robin—because by the time he was back from the rest room, she was gone.

At the stand that business in Harris's book that had him settling down in two years was okay for bullshit during work, but that was all. At five Highspire and Cooper packed up. Cooper tried dragging the stand solo. He damn near made it all the way. You bend, put your arms behind, and lift up on the crossbeams, then tilt the stand onto your back and drag like hell. It took very strong thighs, broad shoulders, and a lot of latent frustration.

Cooper's wife packed up all her stuff. She got in the car, called out something about leftovers, and pulled out. At that point, Cooper unlocked his bike, straddled it, and walked it over to Ronny.

"You know, Hopkins, I heard about your little trouble today. I know our Julie's only three, but it's people like you—deviates—who make it tough these days to be a parent." With that, Cooper put his feet to the pedals and took off.

The speech pushed Ronny to Peggy's to find out what her problem was. If she was looking for trouble, he'd save her a trip. He got to the house and could see from the front drive that she was in the little backyard on a lounge, reading. U2 blared from inside the house. He went to the front door and knocked. He knew he'd get Linda, and he did. In a bikini.

"Hi."

She took hold of his arm, "Ron." She stood on her toes to be kissed, except she wasn't alone. Four of her friends sat around, smoking cigarettes and passing two-quart bottles of Miller. He smiled at her. She took his arm with both hands, put it around her hip, and brought him into the room. "Everybody, this is Ron."

What a picture. The four kids all stared at him. The three girls looked happy he was interrupting, but the guy looked at him and sat there as if he'd just been shot in the chest, slouching down so his white, hairy legs stuck out in the middle of the room.

"Ron's a lifeguard."

"Wow," snickered the boy. He was skinny with black stubs of whiskers scattered on his chin. The empty spot next to him on the couch was where Linda had been sitting. "You save anybody today?" he smirked.

"Two turtles and a duck. You want them for your tubby time?" Ronny shot back. Then, "Your mom's out there. What kind of mood is she in?"

"Okay." She was back on the couch. A dribble of beer ran down her chin onto her stomach. "You going to see her?"

"Yeah. I wanted to see you, too."

"Aww."

He went out to the kitchen toward the back door. He'd wanted to put more of a damper on the skinny kid's day by playing up to Linda some more, but it was time to face Peggy. Besides, the last thing he wanted was to have her come in and see him toying with her daughter.

He closed the screen door softly so he wouldn't startle her. She brought a hand over her eyes and looked at him for a second, then dropped her book in her lap and sat up.

"Peace mission." He held up both hands and walked toward her.

She took off her sunglasses. "Are those goddamn kids still in the house?"

"They're in there. They Linda's bunch?"

"God, yes. That Tony, the skinny one with the goatee. Have you seen him around or talked to him? He's here all the time. Did you take a good look at that boy?" She shook her head. She had half a smile on her face.

For a second, he forgot the reason he came to her house.

She played with her hair, trying to fluff it out from lying flat against her head. "A full day on the beach. You got some color. A new job and a new tan." She scratched and left long red trails on her arms and the tops of her thighs. "I sit out here roasting and don't get a thing."

"I got your message, your complaint. Casivette delivered it to me in person this afternoon in front of the whole beach." He turned his back to her and started kicking at the grass. He knocked the hell out of a clump of dandelions. The white puffs sailed across the yard. "It's not easy, living the way I want to. People judge you, you know?" He kept shuffling and kicking around her yard, smoking a cigarette and flicking the ash out for effect. "Yeah. It impressed the hell out of Casivette that after two days on the job; I got in some kind of hot water. I don't think he was too thrilled."

"I filed a complaint, for God's sake. I had to. What was I going to tell the cop after I called? I'm mad at that pervert friend of yours I suppose. What the hell went on over there?"

When he heard that, he knew she wanted his ass. Linda was just an excuse.

She wrapped a towel around herself and started past him toward the door. She stopped on the top step—the music rolled out of the house like smoke— then came back an inch away from his face.

"I had to tell Linda it was about her. I'm not having her believe what she likes about being in a spot like that with that freaky creep. I had to show her it's the wrong goddamn thing to get herself into."

Things were working out. He followed her into the kitchen and watched her take glasses down from the cupboard. She'd thrown the towel across a chair. She had to stretch up to reach the glasses. Her ass tightened under her suit.

"Look, I didn't mean to say that about Jimmy, but can you put yourself in my shoes?" She started fixing two screwdrivers.

"Sure, I can. With a house and a kid to raise?"

"Those kids. Don't they have homes?" She made a move for the door out to the living room.

"Forget them."

She turned around. He checked the time. He told himself to get the hell out of there. He'd made peace, and he didn't need to be in the kitchen with Peggy and her high-hipped tank suit. She had the same bottle of Gordon's vodka he'd brought over a couple weeks ago.

"You like screwdrivers, don't you? It's a good, cool drink after a day on the beach. It's healthy."

The music had stopped. He took a drink. "Maybe you should check on Linda."

 She banged shut the refrigerator door. "Every goddamn thing you say is Linda, Linda, Linda. You don't mention anyone else! Linda this, Linda that. Go see her if you're curious. Go see!" She pounded up the back kitchen stairway. Ice splashed out of her drink and bounced down the steps.

It stayed quiet in the front room for a few seconds. Then the stereo came back on—Madonna—much softer now. The little hedonists must have been eavesdropping.

He called up the stairway, "I am what I am and that's all that I am."

The stereo quit again, and from the front room came Linda's voice. "You're Popeye the sailor man, *toke! toke!*"

He stuck his head through the doorway. There was Linda, standing by the stereo receiver, smiling.

"You remembered my motto."

"I remembered the cartoon."

Tony the tough tried his best to ignore Ronny, but the others laughed. He went back into the kitchen to chug his drink and leave when Peggy called him from upstairs.

"Ron."

"I'm still here."

That kept up for a good minute. The stereo came back to life, and then, he heard, "Come on up." It seemed like an expedient thing to do.

She sat in her favorite chair watching TV. The chair was big enough to swallow her, and she had her legs tucked underneath, wearing a sundress with no suit underneath.

"I did it again."

"It's Saturday night," he held up his glass. She looked away from the screen, kept her eyes on him while her toe traced circles on the chair's arm.

"You look like Willie off the pickle boat."

He told himself he'd make the Commodore by eight as he knelt on the floor. He figured an hour at the most including shower, two block walk and then a quick change—he had it in the back of his mind as he held his screwdriver to Peggy's mouth and helped her sip. A drop ran down her cheek and throat, and he kissed the trail.

Later in the shower, Peggy wondered out loud, "What can we do tonight?"

"We've done it."

They were watching TV when they heard the ice cream man going past outside. They were lying on the floor wrapped in blankets, the pillows from the chair under their heads.

"Let's stop him." He scrambled to the window, "Stop!"

The driver didn't crack a smile when Peggy and Ronny walked out of that house together wrapped in blankets. They checked selections; the driver checked his watch.

"God forbid if twenty kids come out of the neighboring houses and give you some business," Peggy told him.

"His shift is done."

Not his shift, his freezer unit. A kid came from somewhere and ordered right away. Mr. Ice Cream rewarded his promptness by serving him immediately, but when he tried to hand the kid his pint of pistachio, the kid dropped it. It hit the street—and stuck. It didn't move, didn't bounce. The kid picked it up. The container was smushed where it hit the pavement.

The kid pointed, "Your stuff's melted! I'm not paying for that!"

Walking back to the house, Ronny's strawberry shortcake almost fell right off the stick. He and Peggy both had a good laugh.

He left Peggy's before dark. The damp night air hit him on her front porch. He jogged to Ocean Ave, ran to the Commodore where he went in the delivery entrance, cut through the small kitchen and up the back stairs. He stopped just in front of his room. The hallway was empty. Only a line of light under a door across the hallway broke the monotony—that and the exit lights.

An idea ran through his head. Travel through the season; try to get everything out of it before it screeched to a halt after Labor Day. He went into his room, turned on the overhead, and all at once, he lost the waves, the boards, and the music on the radio. He stood in the middle of that room, looked around at the black floor and the furnishings, and thought what thirty-three-year-old would bring Robin in here?

He had no idea what he was in for. He didn't even change. He just walked down to the lobby. There sat Robin in the Engine Room at a corner table, watching everybody come and go. She didn't spot him right away. She craned her neck, then looked down and checked her watch.

He walked over to her. "I'm late."

She stood up and hugged him. She kept holding him. "I just got here." She held onto him there in the Engine Room. Only one straw was next to her drink, and the ice still packed the glass. He stepped back to look at her, and then he picked her up in his arms and spun her around.

"Hopkins!"

They talked about ordering something to eat before he realized he had to change.

"I'll be back in a flash."

"Out with the boys after work for a few beers?"

"I have a room upstairs."

"You told me before. How convenient. So get going," she smiled.

Walking away, he looked back and saw her single face and figure. Her eyes stuck on him as people passed between. He stood in that one spot in the lobby for a moment before he went back to her.

"You like swings?"

She tipped her chin to one side.

"Let's get out of here."

She got up, and he walked her out the door and down the street. It was twilight. The boardwalk lights were misty balls. Only a few people sauntered past them.

"The sand's going to be a little damp."

"Why are you talking so loud?"

"These are great swings we're going to."

On the ramp past the gate, they kicked off their shoes. On top, the sand had wet skin. It was damp underneath. He weighed it in his palm.

"It's heavy like it rained."

"It did rain. A quick shower. You were inside with your bar friends."

Their feet turned up dry tracks in the sand. On the swings, he pulled back hard on the chains to start out. He had to bend and swing his legs to one side, so they didn't drag. Air swooshed through the chains when he leaned forward and back, pulling like hell. Robin watched him let go and fly off in mid-swing, then laughed when he ran out the jump and made believe he tripped.

"Did you get it all out of your system?"

"I think so," brushing himself off.

"You never know." Hands locked together, her elbows held the chains. "You just can't be still, can you?"

"I sit still all day."

"I saw you today, bouncing around on the stand, climbing up, jumping down." Car lights swung around a corner, reached over their heads and down Ocean Ave. He sat down on his swing and started pumping the chains.

"Going for the big drop—past the jumping point, past horizontal." At the top of his arc, he let the chains go slack and dropped straight down. On his ass in the wet sand, the swing twisted and rattled behind him. "All out now. Let's go. First to the Commodore kitchen, then to the lake. We're going to Silver Lake to feed the ducks."

She looked at him. "Feed the ducks?"

"Do you fish? Feeding the ducks is almost the same thing, except better. When you fish, you sit and wait a lot. You hope for a bite. And if you're lucky, you catch something. Now, what's the best part about catching something?"

"Eating it," she played along.

"No, seeing it up close. Why do you think people go to the zoo? You can buy fish and eat them. Feeding ducks eliminates wait, luck, and calories. First back to the Commodore for stale bread."

At the lake with a nice loaf, they found a bench, and Robin started right in. She threw a few pieces. To lure them over Ronny lobbed pebbles. After a few minutes, a pair of mallards came over, then a big white duck and two swans. Some ducklings showed up with momma, and Robin coaxed them up the concrete incline.

"You have to like a town that puts that much money into aiding its duck population."

"You're good with them. Are you good with people like that, too? You must be—you're a nurse."

"People aren't ducks," she laughed.

"Yeah, they're a little more trouble. Like me."

"You're as much trouble as you want to be, or as little."

He put down his bread, sat down on the ground and leaned back with his hands behind his head. For a second, he thought the ground was too damp. He looked past her at the cars running along Ocean Ave.

"You want to talk, that's fine. We can talk sports or politics. I'll tell you about one team, and you can tell me about another. But none of that being more trouble shit. I don't know a thing about that right now. Nothing. In a year or five, maybe. I'll be able to see it. Not right now."

A car with a stereo cranking drove by, and Robin got on one knee. "You know all about it. You brought it up, remember? You wouldn't have said anything about trouble if you didn't have that speech all set. You can't stand by anything or anybody without that excuse, then it's off you go by yourself." She jumped up. "Why the hell don't you move out to that island? *Live* with the damn ducks. Build a swing out there."

Her loaf was gone. She looked over the water for a long time without talking. She sat down with her arms around her knees, every so often rocking back and forth, bending her head down.

He smoked a cigarette. He had no intention of talking. He was surprised he was still there, for God's sake. Then that car with the stereo came around again, and this time when it passed them, it slowed down.

"Okay. Where are you staying tonight?" He took his room key and safety pin off his rowing shorts and tossed them. "Take it. It's my room key. You can stay there tonight, and I'll stay at Jimmy's, and we'll chalk this up to experience."

She looked down at the key for a second. "Is that what you want?"

Behind her on the boardwalk, he could see the lights of the Lake Ave Pavilion. On Saturday nights in the summer, the town had senior socials there—dancing to the big band sounds. Only a five- or six-piece band, but they tried.

He walked to where he'd tossed the key and picked it up. "No, that's not what I want. What I'd like to do is go dancing down at the pavilion," he pointed. "How about it?"

He guided her with fingertips. They started down the lake path toward the pavilion. As they walked, the sound of the band became clearer through the traffic and fog.

She gripped his hand, "Is that the place?"

"I hope it's not too late, that we can get a few dances in."

They stepped into that big, bright pavilion, and he saw right away that things were about to end. It was eleven o'clock according to the old guy at the door who looked Ronny up and down.

"Not exactly dressed for the occasion, are you, Bub? We're closing." He was all decked out in a pale blue suit with white tasseled loafers and white belt to match.

Ronny took a twenty out of his rowing shorts pocket and held it out for him. "C'mon, we're in love."

Robin yanked his arm trying to go back through the doorway. The band, the whole place watched them.

Ronny requested, "How about "Begin the Beguine?" I know that one six pieces or sixty."

The blue suit handed the twenty to the accordion player. They hit "Begin the Beguine."

He didn't pull her close and just circle like high school kids. He saw people he recognized.

The music sputtered to a stop. They didn't move. They were the last couple on the floor. The rest of the people milled around the doorways, chatting, touching one another's arms and saying good night. Robin looked up at him as the pavilion emptied around them.

"A most pleasant dance, sir."

He walked her down the boardwalk to her car. Before she got in, he kissed her.

"I'm staying with a friend on Sussex. You know something about caring."

He called out, "Come to the beach tomorrow."

A car full of schoolgirls heard him. They stuck their fat arms out the windows, banged them against the doors, waved and smiled, and called out things. Walking back to my place, he lit a cigarette. The matches were damp, and he broke two off before he got one to flame. It was still misting out, but he couldn't figure out why the matches were so damp. He tucked them into his back pocket, and his hand came away wet. He brought his hand up to his face. He knew the smell. All that time at the pavilion, he slow danced at a senior citizen social with algae-ass from where he sat at the lake.

12

T HE BOROUGH BOYS skipped a pile, eh?"

The algae accumulate and tangle with litter along the lake's edge. It gets scooped out by hand. The borough has a crew equipped with box-shaped wire nets.

I pictured the lake at night. Not many people around. The lamplights along the path that winds around the lake reflect off the surface so that when a breeze blows, the whole lake sparkles. Houses around the lake are lit up, and there isn't a bar within a block. Two big places are lit up, almost at either end of the lake. One is a hotel, the Barclay, which caters to parties, proms, and what not. The other is Kenmore funeral home. Ronny's father's service was there. I'll never forget all the people, the cars parked all around the lake, the cop whistles tooting at traffic, re-routing it.

The phone rang. I got up and picked up the receiver. Talking on the phone is tricky. I have to hold my voice and the receiver apart, so they don't fuzz each other up. For a second there was nothing on the line. Then a heavy female voice, as if disguised, started groaning.

"Ron Hopkins?"

"For you." I handed it to him.

"Hello. Hello? Who is this? Never mind? Never mind who?" A few seconds passed, and Ronny cracked up. He fell over in the chair, laughing, then handed me the phone.

"It must be for you, buddy. Somebody wants to fuck your brains out."

I hung it up. "Peggy?"

"Who else?"

I swirled my drink. All the ice had melted. "You remembered my duck theory."

I have a duck-feeding guide for prospective girlfriends. Everything about a girl can be discovered by how she feeds ducks. Before the first crumb's thrown, there's the selection of the bread. If there's a choice, a solid loaf is best. Sliced bread is too easy to chuck one slice at a time. Then there's the breaking of the bread. Stale bread works best because it floats a little longer, but you have to be careful because when it's thrown, the wind can carry it.

That's number one. The intelligent woman uses stale bread that's been dipped in the lake. Not soaked—dipped. As far as breaking off pieces goes, she should conserve. Number two, she shouldn't tear off a fistful and chuck it out there because if ten ducks stab their beaks at one huge hunk, there's no telling what'll get pecked. It also eliminates the less aggressive ducks. It's not fair. That kind of woman is the last thing you want. Number three, if she's in a hurry, she thinks the whole idea is ridiculous and a waste of time, which means *you* are wasting *your* time. You're there, she's there. Why rush? No, the bread should be broken off, one duck-sized bite at a time, and fed to them slowly. No shotgun style. And it counts where she throws the bread. Last, some women pick out a certain duck and keep feeding it—even worse, she picks out a swan. Unless you're a swan, you may want to reconsider.

"And Jimmy, Robin attracted those ducklings like a pro, shared the wealth among them, and made sure one didn't get left out or beaten to every piece tossed."

"I'm going to bed."

"Still the weekend tomorrow."

"It's Sunday today. Go to bed."

Sunday, rain or shine, was the big day in Belmar—the last chance for Joe or Jane Benny to make a romantic connection. On Sunday, Joe and Jane shopped. First thing, maybe an ocean-swim Bloody Mary. They might stick with that all day if they liked. They could head to a restaurant and for coffee and a hard roll, maybe mimosas and eggs Benedict. Or of course a bar. If the weekend had been a fast, Sunday would have been the last chance to grab something from the Belmar buffet. That or the lies would fly in Monday's carpool.

Sunday is the day I call Alice and talk to her and the kids. She has two little ones, three and five, both girls—Jessica and Suzanne. As I said Alice's husband, their father, no longer permits any more than phone contact between me and his daughters. I try to call between four and five o'clock. At nearly four, the clouds inland and overhead started to swell.

I'd just about given up seeing either Peggy or Robin when I spotted Highspire walking Robin down the beach. She wore jeans with a tank top and carried sandals. People seemed to be clearing a path for them—they folded blankets, packed odd items. The first sign of dark clouds on a Sunday means tavern or take-off time.

Ronny hit the bullhorn then, "Get away from her, Highspire. Take your hands off my sister."

People turned to look. Highspire dropped a step behind Robin and went around to the other side of the stand away from her and Ronny.

"You're just in time for the clouds," Ronny said.

Her hair blew across her forehead. She reached up and brushed it back. "Hi, Jimmy, gentlemen." Then to Ronny, "Sorry I'm late. My friends and I were feeding ducks."

"I'll bet."

"It's true; we were. We only stopped for a minute, though. Some of them had to get back home."

"How about you?"

She shrugged. He put a hand on her shoulder.

"I'm off all week. One week on, one week off."

"We were packed today before the clouds hit." He looked at her. "Are you staying for a while?"

She looked out at the water and dug little trenches in the sand with her feet. She stooped and picked up a plastic baggie blowing across the sand. "I don't know."

"Sunday's the best night of the week."

"I don't know."

"Look, a few of us are stopping at the Tropical. You know it?"

"On Waterfront?" she laughed. "I've been past it. The roof sags."

"Stop by if you're up for it."

She said, "Okay" just as thunder boomed—all guards' favorite song.

"Ladies and gentlemen, thunder has been heard…"

She jogged up the beach to the boards, and Ronny helped me pack up. He shoved my thermos into my backpack. "Anticipation and I don't get along."

"You were hoping she'd come by."

He smiled.

"Let's *go!*" Highspire yelled.

The scramble started. In the southwest, the clouds stacked up like a rack of eight balls. Another rumble rolled from a distance, then split the air down the coast. Ronny and Vinny ran the boat up the beach; Harris, Cooper, and Highspire took care of the equipment. People scurried up to the boardwalk into cars. Trunks popped open all along Ocean Ave. Annie with her umbrella was long gone. I dumped my stuff into the guard's storage bin.

"You going to make it?" A big rip cracked overhead, and I swore my feet left the road crossing Ocean Ave. Ronny, Vinny, Harris, and I crammed into Harris' car. We weren't in the car ten seconds when the rain started. It knocked against the roof at first then came down in sheets. The windows fogged sealing us in a gray cloud.

Vinny snickered, "Don't you die, Jimmy."

"Can't get my breath," I puffed. "Too tight in here," I rolled down my window.

"Vinny's kidding. He wants your booze stash. What is this, Harris? This is new," Ronny said.

"Toyota Corolla." Harris picked out tunes.

I turned and looked at the speakers mounted behind the back seat about a foot from my ears. Too late. The steering wheel turned into a snare, the rearview mirror a cymbal, and the rest of the dash a tom-tom. After two songs so loud they hurt my teeth, I decided to take my chances with the lightning.

The storm had turned into a light shower—steady, a few flashes of lightning cutting into the gray distance over the water. The boardwalk looked slick and dark. Down Ocean Ave steam drifted up from the blacktop. I heard a rumble, but the storm had blown way out to sea, so I climbed up on the boardwalk. The fat, white trash cans on the beach looked like sentries standing out in some battle's haze. Cars swished through puddles waiting their turn at the storm drain. The air felt gloriously lighter.

I heard a car door close. Ronny came alongside me with a cigarette. I took a hit. The smoke burned hot and dry in my throat because I'd thrown my filter out the window of Harris' sound machine. I gagged.

"That bad, huh?"

I just shook my head.

"You heard that conversation I had with Robin. What the hell did I say? Stop by?"

"Please come with me would have been my choice instead of 'stop by.'"

"I'm not up for rehearsing a new part when I can act out an old one with my eyes closed." He stared out at the water. Not a soul out on the sand—even the gulls had cleared out. "Come on," he nudged me, "we're going to the Tropical."

The Tropical is on Waterfront—thirteen beautiful blocks away. "I'm up for anything." Every time my body tells me I'm not twenty-five anymore, I let it know I'm still boss. We walked to Harris's car.

"Tell Highspire, if he comes back, that I came down with something— no, tell him I had to take Jimmy home for a new filter. See?" Ronny pointed at my stoma.

Harris stared like Nicklaus eyeing a putt.

Vinny said, "Hoppy, Hoppy, what's up?"

"See you at the Tropical. That's what's up."

13

WE TOOK A few detours on the way to the Tropical. We stopped at J's Corner where the owner, Mr. Lippmann—a taller version of a leprechaun better known as the Lipp—gave us a wink and let Ronny change from his new guard gear into jeans and a collared shirt. Then up to A Street because Ronny didn't want Casivette or Highspire spotting him away from the beach. At my place, Ronny stashed his new sweats and I changed. I had a shower and I talked Ronny into calling us a cab, too. The hell with those thirteen blocks.

I thought about calling Alice, but I wasn't in the mood for her husband's routine. I can't understand you, who is this? He knows who it is, the bastard. He does it every time before he hands the phone over to Alice.

The rain had just about quit. Ronny talked about stopping at Estel's, but I could see from the cab through the big picture window that the place was packed. The marquee read "Scarlet Begonias."

"I love those guys," Ronny said.

"That means a cover and many out-of-state residents.

You'll never make the Tropical. Robin at the Tropical."

We kept going.

There's a MacDonald's on the boardwalk at Waterfront. It sits inside the same, beautiful old pavilion where my father smoked his cigars on summer nights.

Memories can be rocks in a farmer's field. The town sold the pavilion a few years ago. Now it's a boutique *and* Ronald's house. The cab dropped us there.

We had a burger and a cup of coffee before we hit the Tropical. Good thing we did. The Tropical was still on their afternoon schedule, so there was no band yet, but as we walked in the bouncers were just cleaning up after a

85

slight disturbance. I talked to one named Al. I met him again later, up close, and personal, as ABC Sports used to say.

"What happened?"

Al swept up broken glass. "A guy didn't like the empties on the stage and fuckin' bowled 'em over with a barstool."

"Did he fly?"

"As far as I wanted."

What a spot to meet a girl.

The jukebox roared as we wadded into the three deep crowd around the front bar. We got two beers. If we'd wanted to catch up to most of the customers, we would've ordered a fifth of grain alcohol. Rainy Sundays will do that.

"I know those people by the jukebox," said Ronny. One of them drained his drink, and I hit Ronny's arm. We squeezed our way over there.

Ronny put a hand on the guy's stool. "You leaving, buddy?"

"Fuck yeah. Good luck."

Eyes along the bar dropped down to my stoma. I held on to Ronny's arm. "I'm glad I have you as insurance." I pushed the money left on the bar into the well if for no other reason than to make another honest friend along the row of screaming faces. Thankfully, I knew Stevie Hughes, the bartender—we call him Wonder—and he spotted me right away.

"Seamus, Ronny. I thought you were going to the Keys, man." His voice is gravel from all the yelling and smoke.

"You didn't hear? I'm working again."

"You're kidding," Wonder poured us three shots of peppermint schnapps. "Congratulations." We clinked and drank. "How's your boy, Casivette?"

"He's the one who asked me back."

"Fuckin' amazing!" Wonder took off.

That was the only conversation until a little after six o'clock when Vinny and a few of the guards from Mercer came in. Sally, a girl guard, was with them. She's some swimmer. I spent that entire time sipping, watching people and thinking, what am I doing in here? I felt like a first-time driver on the Turnpike. Too many cars going too goddamn fast.

"Here he is," Vinny said with his hand on Ronny's shoulder, "the fugitive."

"Highspire miss me?"

"He never came back. Hoppy, you won't believe it. Cooper's coming."

"Go on. On a Sunday?"

"His wife showed up an' they sat in her car an' then he got out, slammed the door, an' went back on a beach. There's trouble in paradise."

Vinny bought us all a round. He sized up the crowd, and then started throwing the bull to the boys from Mercer.

"I can hypnotize any girl to buy me a beer." He made sure he had his new sweats just right. Two girls walked by, Vinny opened his eyes wide and brought both hands, fingers doing Bela Lugosi, up to his face. He bobbed his head like a fighter ducking jabs, all the time focusing on the girl and swaying his hips. The girls cracked up and walked away.

I wasn't interested in Vinny. I saw a break in the crowd and got up to go to the bathroom. When I came back, some guys were standing at my stool. My change was still on the bar, and by reflex, I checked my pockets. I had my voice, but my wallet was missing. For the life of me, I couldn't remember where I'd had it or seen it last. Did I dump it into the guard bin with my beach stuff? Have it in Harris's car? Have it in the apartment when we stopped there?

I walked over to Ronny. "You see my wallet on the bar?"

He laughed, watching Vinny's hypno thing.

I stepped between him and Vinny. "Ronny, my wallet. Do you know where it is?"

He saw the look on my face. "Okay, okay. Where'd you leave it? On the bar?" He looked at the guards from Mercer. "Any of you see a wallet? It's black, right, Jimmy? Any of you see a black wallet?" He went from one guy to the next, asking each one of them. I stood there and rocked back and forth on my heels. A girl talking to Vinny stared at me.

I didn't say anything to anybody on my way out of the Tropical. Outside I sat on the curb and lit a cigar. I had to stand and move because some idiot wanted to parallel park his minivan in a space too small for a VW. I kept thinking about the things I had in my wallet, the pictures I had tucked away in it.

The alcohol did most of the thinking. It thought it remembered putting the wallet in my back pocket at home. One of two things had happened. Somebody had picked me clean, or somebody had lifted it off the bar. I'd been drinking beer and peppermint schnapps, so I didn't think single-malt thoughts.

I pushed my way back into the bar past, through, and around the people waiting to go in. Evening had arrived. Soon the band would crank up. People wanted to beat the cover. Ronny stood where I left him.

"Anybody find it?"

"Here," he handed me a twenty. "Relax. You probably didn't bring it."

"I want my wallet." I took hold of his arm. "We're going to look for it."

We got Vinny, and all three of us walked up and down the bar where we'd been before I went to the bathroom. I got down on my hands and knees—on that floor not a smart move. I made my way over to the stage, grabbed the microphone, and handed it to Ronny.

"If anybody finds a black wallet," he said, "it's mine. There's a forty-dollar reward." He held up two twenties.

I had a drink hoping someone with my wallet would come up to me and say, surprise! The band started and I couldn't hear myself think. People were having conversations like those flamingoes that dip, get a drink, and tip back up. Ronny leaned to talk to Vinny; Vinny stretched to talk back.

Then I had an idea where to look. I went into the men's room and dumped the trashcan all over the floor. I sifted through a mess of paper, bottles, and who knows what. Nothing.

Then I went into the woman's room. About ten girls waiting for a stall screamed, "Get the hell out of here!"

I ignored them. I dumped the trash, and there sat my black wallet in white paper towels and toilet paper bundles.

I had my wallet in my back pocket when Al and another bouncer came in. I went with them—didn't even try to resist.

Al sent me through the doorway with, "Goodbye, dearie. Don't come back tonight." He didn't push me. Let's just say he propelled me.

After a few steps outside on the grass, I heard, "Jimmy!"

It was Robin. She and her friend stood at the end of the door line.

I walked back to her. I managed to wave toward the place. I mouthed, "Ronny," and pointed at the door.

"Are you okay? What's the matter? Why are you out of breath?" She waited for an answer. She turned and looked at her friend, a girl with long, dark hair who swiveled her head around as if she expected somebody to jump out from a bush and cut her throat.

"I'll be right back, Lisa. Stay right there." Robin left the line—her friend Lisa holding the spot—and took me over onto neighboring steps and sidewalk where people stood talking. It was cooler than in the bar, no smoke, and a hell of a lot quieter.

"Where to start?" I lit a cigar. "How the hell would you like to live here?" I threw a thumb back at the house behind us and shook my head. "I got tossed out of the Tropical."

She stretched her legs out straight, leaned back on her hands. "It's too crowded for you. You'll do a lot better with a protector over your stoma. You don't need to be taking in that smoke, with or without protection."

"You're the nurse." I put the cigar out in the grass. "Better? You're a good nurse."

"Robin, Robin, I'm almost in." Lisa had moved up the steps and onto the porch, almost to the door.

"Go ahead, save her. She's scared to death." I walked Robin to Lisa.

After they went inside, I sat down and stretched back. I couldn't have been there five minutes when Al, the door stud, left his post, came down from the porch and paddy-caked my head a few times.

"Hey, buddy. Huh. You again. You can't sleep here. C'mon. You gotta go, man. Go home."

I sat up, took a deep breath. Al stood there until I got up. He went back to his door, and I started home. I felt my empty wallet in my back pocket—no cab fare.

My walk did not go well. I couldn't hold a course, and I didn't want some cop on Ocean Ave writing me up for a PI, so I cut down to A Street and then headed north. After you get nailed for public intoxication a few times, such things become second nature even when you're rolling. I had to walk around the tip of Silver Lake, but what the hell.

With the apartment building in sight, I started singing Sam Cooke in my head. Sam Cooke bringin' it on home. Up the stairs I went. Clothes dropped along the way. Inside I looked at the clock—nine thirty-six. What a big night. I opened the refrigerator and stared in. I sat down cross-legged on the floor, my knee propping the refrigerator door, inspecting Tupperware containers stacked like building blocks. I opened the biggest one. It held something thick and heavy. I stuck a finger in and tasted—pancake batter from that morning.

I put on the griddle, melted butter, poured, and waited for them to fluff up, light and hot. Old batter doesn't rise—I got flat jacks instead of flapjacks. I tried flipping a couple and wound up with pancake nuggets. I found some bacon and cooked that right on the griddle. On the pile of nuggets went syrup, butter, and blueberries mashed with my Kitchen Wand. I watched TV while I ate. I heard a car door slam; people yelled in the street. I got up, turned everything off, and went to bed.

I couldn't sleep. Robin's story had been sweet—I shouldn't have been such a smart ass. Her advice about my stoma had me thinking back to the time right after my surgery. What a royal pain. I treated those nurses as if they personally stole my larynx. I didn't want to hear anything about laryngectomy tubes, shower shields, forceps, or saline misters. I didn't take good care of my stoma, and I didn't want some fancy ascot to cover it up. Every time I started to talk, the EL and that distinctive *click* made my situation too obvious for my liking. At least I'd finished that phase.

That night should have been my cut-off, my slow down. I had a big week—met new people; found new friends—every one of them young and attractive. New names swirled in my head. Hometown streets sounded more real. Events came to me so fast… It dazzled me after my lonely winter, and I lost track of where I was in life, of what mattered.

When you're chest deep in rough water, sometimes you're not the best judge of whether it's time to swim to shore.

14

MONDAY MORNING I took a shower—yes, with my shower guard on. I let the water run hard and cool against my back, over my head, and thought about spending some money. The mess in the kitchen could wait.

First my cab stopped at the bank so I could check my accounts. Then out along Rt.35 to Shore Cadillac, just this side of Asbury. I had a friend out there who ran the body shop. On his desk sat an aerosol can that read **Bullshit Repellant**—my kind of guy.

Depending on who you ask, Caddy fins were caput after 1964. Others say they continued for years. Those were baby fins, the shape of the taillights, if you ask me. I found a black Coupe de Ville convertible with black leather seats. Skirts? Of course. No white walls, though. That would have been too much to ask. The tires had plenty of tread. Under the hood: the monster 429 cu in V-8, 340 hp, new for '64. Seven liters. Probably got eight miles a gallon. The body looked in good shape. Even better, the convertible top was in one piece. I took her for a drive.

She rode like a big, fat dinosaur. They could have asked for two million, and if I'd had it, they'd have gotten it.

Monday was Highspire's day off, which meant Ronny topped Inlet's totem pole. I was curious about how things had gone with Robin at the Tropical, but I didn't rush to get down there. Clouds hung low as Belmar dozed from the weekend. There would be plenty of time to catch up on things. I stopped at J's for a bagel and coffee before I hit the boards.

Ronny stood at the gate with Annie. He saw me coming, and he pointed and talked to Annie as I walked up. I heard "…was unbelievable. Batter dripping down cabinets. Grease on the floor so think I could skate. Spatters—"

91

"What's he telling you, Annie?"

"Oh, my goodness. You don't want to know."

"He keeps breaking into my apartment to use my facilities. The common commode at the Commodore isn't good enough for him."

"The jokester has arrived. Well, Jimmy here looks like a model citizen, but he's a sexual predator who hides in women's restrooms."

"No way, Annie."

"That's right. You just barge right in. What time did you get up and out? I was at the scene of the pancake slaughter about eight."

"Early enough. Today it's your beach. Highspire's off, right?"

"Oh, that boy," Annie said.

"He'll learn." I pointed at Ronny. "Like this one has to."

We both stared at Ronny. "Don't give the Captain any guff. Remember, I have police power today."

Ronny took the paddleboard out of the storage locker. I walked alongside him toward the stand. He put the paddleboard on his head and turned to me. "Here we are. Endless summer and endless munch."

When I saw the water, I knew why he wanted the paddleboard. It wasn't rough in the sense of heavy surf, but I could tell from the scum trails—froth from pounding waves that builds up—and the way the high-tide wash moved across the shoreline that there was a wicked north-south run.

I spread my towel on the other side of the Benny rope above the tide line and buried all four corners so the wind wouldn't sail it. A roller came up just as I wiped off my hands. It reached the damn towel and bubbled away into the sand.

"Moon tide." Ronny picked up my towel.

"You see Robin at the Tropical last night?"

"Don't ask."

I looked at him and held up both hands.

"I don't know. Her friend was there with her."

"So?"

"She glued herself to Robin's hip. They were a pain in the ass."

A pain in the ass. "We should all have such pain." I watched him squeeze the water out of my towel. I wanted to snatch the son of a bitch from him, but I waited. He handed me my towel, and I went around to the back of the stand and tossed it over a crossbeam.

Cooper came down the beach. He collapsed in the stand's shade spot with a bottle of apple juice. He didn't look so hot.

"Bad night?"

He chugged some juice. "A tiff with my missus."

"Tell Jimmy what you tolme, Coopa," Vinny said. "He tolme his wife drove 'em to find solstice in alcohol."

"*Solace.* God, you're an idiot."

Vinny winked at me and chanted, "Coopa, Coopa, Coopa."

Ronny's and Vinny's horseshit got to me. I walked up to Annie's gate—she was on break, and I talked to Harvey Schecterman for a while. Harvey was a DG— designated gateman. He traveled from gate to gate to give the regulars their breaks. Sometimes he worked the gate down on Seaside where all the fifteen-year-olds hung out. He was a nifty, short Jew with bushy dark hair and a quick smile.

"What's it doing down there, Mr. Seamus?"

"Gloomy. The tide's mixed up, the clouds are keeping everyone away, and the water's cold and choppy. Soon, you'll have no work."

"Young man, where is your beach badge? It's not clearly visible."

"You're wearing your hat bill-backwards now like the kids on your beach? Isn't there an age limit on that?" Harvey is Ronny's age.

"Tomorrow I'm on Seaside all day. All those kids." He took off his hat, looked at it, and put it back on backwards. "The water's been cold all year. You went to the Tropical with Ronny last night? He said Wonder worked."

"Wonder worked. You remember playing on Kiwanis in little league? You stole second base one game and slid high and hard into George Clarkson. You broke Georgie's glasses."

"I went in too high, not too hard. Never too hard."

"Your seventh-grade year, Belmar Elementary. Who played every position?"

"*Seventh* grade?"

"Second base?"

"Me." Harvey backhanded an imaginary grounder and flipped to first.

After Harvey, I went home. I didn't want to miss the phone call about my Caddy. I got anxious, and to keep myself busy decided to start my tomato sauce—tomato gravy my Italian friends called it—for my lasagna.

I had my sauce at simmer stage when I got the call from Shore Cadillac. "The car checked out okay. All the fluid levels are good. You'll need some brake work done soon, and the shocks, too, but you're good to go."

I took a shower to get the salt and sand off, dressed, and took a cab—my last cab—up to Asbury to pick up my new car.

First, I set the seat. I never had a car with power seats. I got the mirrors adjusted, settled back into the leather, and put down the armrest—the big fat kind right in the seat's middle.

"You aren't going to get much cool flow," the sales guy cautioned. "The AC needs to be charged, and that gets tricky with these older systems."

"Tricky is a euphemism for expensive." I held up a finger, hit the top's switch, and watched as it lifted, folded, and settled. I smiled. "Never drove a convertible before." Pulling out of Shore Cadillac onto 35, I goosed that 429. She roared into the left lane where she belonged.

All that moving air—I was glad I had a filter over my stoma. It was hard getting a breath sometimes, but I discovered that if I sat forward a little, I could tolerate the air that hit me square on. I still cut east to get off 35 at the Neptune City Mall. I wanted a nice, slow ride along the ocean.

At a light, I remembered I could move the seat up with the touch of a finger. That tickled the hell out of me. Everything did, especially driving with the open sky overhead. That drop-top supplied instant therapy. Along the beach, it got even better. No wonder convertibles inspired songs.

It was close to five o'clock when I parked on Ocean Ave across the street from Inlet. There were empty spaces along the boardwalk, but I didn't want Annie or any of the guards to see me pull up. I walked across the street to the gate just as Harris ran up the beach. Harvey still manned the gate—Annie had left for the day—and Harris came up to me and shook my hand like I was a priest.

"Sorry about Saturday, man."

"That was two days ago."

"I was fuckin' out of it yesterday," he laughed.

"Let me show you something."

I took him across the street and showed him the Caddy.

He hopped in it and asked me all kinds of questions I couldn't answer about transmission ratios and torque. He knew more about the car than I did. "This is one fine ride, Jimmy." He brushed sand from his rowing shorts off the leather, and we walked back across Ocean Ave just in time to see his majesty the Captain.

"Let's get back to work, Harris. Jimmy, you seen Casivette's pickup this afternoon?"

"Highspire's dead. Long live the Captain."

"I'll take that as a no. I was sure he'd be around before closing."

"Ask Harvey." Harvey picked his nose up out of the *Daily News*.

"Haven't seen him. Jimmy, that's your car?" he looked across the street. "That's a *nice* car. A fun car for the beach. Where'd you get that?"

"Take five minutes to see my new car." Harvey and Ronny followed me over to her. Ronny stood on the sidewalk with his arms folded.

"It's a battleship. An aircraft carrier with black leather bench seats."

"It drives," I smiled and moved a flat hand in a straight line. I raised the hood. Ronny and Harvey walked around the car as if they were kids eyeing a Christmas morning package. I smiled at their smiles. When I glanced down Ocean Ave and spotted the roof of Casivette's pickup sticking up above the line of traffic coming north, all I had to do was point.

"Shit."

Ronny took off across the street and jumped onto the boardwalk, except he didn't quite make it. On the way up his right foot caught the boardwalk's edge. He went down hard on his left side, and then rolled over onto his butt, holding his foot. Harvey and I crossed.

A big, jagged splinter had gone through the ball of Ronny's foot from behind the toe and out toward the arch. It looked as if somebody had stuck a Popsicle stick through a plum.

Harris brought the first aid box from the stand, and then there was Casivette standing over Ronny, looking down like Achilles over Hector's corpse.

"Anybody watching the water? The judges are giving you a seven on the fall, Hopkins. I'm giving you a five. We'll have to see about your working."

Soon a little crowd gathered around Ronny. They didn't say anything, just pointed and whispered. Ronny hopped over to a bench and held up his foot. "Five dollars a picture."

I lit a cigarette and handed it to him. "Pose with this."

Casivette got back in his truck. Nice and loud he called, "Have somebody take you to Doc Lukens. Tell Doc who you are. If you were where you were supposed to be, you wouldn't have had to sprint across Ocean when you saw me coming."

Cooper came up from the stand. He studied the foot. "You'll need to get that wood cut away a bit at a time." He cocked his head, checked all the angles. For a second I thought Ronny would kick his face.

"Get me a towel, Cooper. Analytical douchebag."

"I'll pull the Caddy around." When I swung in, Ronny wrapped the towel around his foot and hopped across the boardwalk. I steered the Caddy into traffic. "Too bad Vinny was on the stand. Guaranteed he would have made a Hoppy joke."

"Hah fuckin' hah."

"Just trying to lighten things up."

I stayed in the waiting room at the doctors. I couldn't believe the language coming out of that office. If I hadn't known better, I would have sworn there was an amputation underway.

After Doc Lukens fixed him up, we stopped uptown at Huxley's Liquors and bought two half-pints of vodka. We had a pull or two in the parking lot. I showed Ronny all the gadgets—power windows, the radio, the wipers.

"What are you, a Cadillac tour guide?"

"What did Lukens say?"

"Keep the bandage and a sock over it and to stay out of the water."

"How are you going to work without swimming?"

He stared straight ahead.

"You'll manage." I pulled out onto Chester. "So why didn't you stick with Robin last night? Because of her friend? You should have *fuck you* tattooed across your forehead."

We got down by the ocean. He put a good hurt on that half-pint, making faces after each drink. He slapped the seat. "How come?"

I shrugged.

"Why'd you buy this car?"

I waved go on at him. I played with every option that Caddy had to offer.

Ronny put his foot on the dash and looked at it. "He packed it with gauze." I saw the bulge of a bandage underneath a white sock. "Keep the sand out of it. No water for a week. That is not happening."

We parked, went up to the apartment, and sat on the balcony. He propped his foot up on the railing, mumbled something, and put it down. I got myself a glass of ice with a little OJ and sat with him. Two seconds later, he motioned at my glass.

"I could go for a set up."

I got him his set up and sat back down. "Propping that keeps the swelling down."

"It'll rush blood poisoning that much faster to my heart, too. What's with the car, Jimmy?"

We touched glasses, or should I say we touched plastic— fifty-fifty vodka screwdrivers in 16oz Burger King Yankee cups.

"See how she catches the light? Even with the cloud cover," I pointed to the Caddy. "She looks sleek with the top down."

"You're going to have to drive me to the Commodore, Jimmy. I'll spend my day off there."

"Fine. I can see you're not a good patient. I could hear, too, at Lukens' office. It sounded like death's agony."

He stuck his foot back up on the railing. "This goddamn thing throbs. I yelled because I screwed myself."

He took a drink, looked down at his cup, picked out a cube, and threw it past his foot.

I wiped a make-believe tear, made a pout face, and threw a cube left-handed like a girl over the railing.

He took a handful of ice, stood up on his good leg, "Three, two, one—" and shot it all like a basketball down at my car. Most of the ice smacked right off the passenger door. "Missed."

"Let me know when you want to get the hell out of here."

"I could use one more set up."

Mother would have been proud. I went into the kitchen, took out my stash, and rolled a nice bone. Then I got him his set up and brought everything back. Down below us most of the beachgoers headed home.

"Good idea." He took a long hit on the bone. "I just noticed watching you how I could see your legs under the fridge door. You were right here when you saw me hitting on Linda, weren't you?"

He had the balls to admit it. He'd met a great girl, spent all day pissing about her, and now made jokes about hitting on a child. "Why would you bring that up?"

"I was thinking about her."

"I don't want to hear your shit. What the hell's wrong with you?"

"Fuck you, daddy! I don't need to listen to this."

He grabbed my voice right out of my hand. I looked at him. He sat there holding my voice, looking out at the street. *The second time he took your voice.*

Something jerked at my heart. I stood up and slapped his arm with the back of my hand. His eyes shot around at me. Still sitting, he clenched a fist. I stepped back, tapped a hand on my neck and mouthed, "It's back. The cancer. In my glands."

Two kids walked below us on the sidewalk. Just off the beach, their towels twirled around like turbans on their heads. I sat down, lit one of my anisette cigars, and let the smoke drift from my mouth. There wasn't a hint of a breeze on that balcony. Not a whisper.

Ronny put my voice back on the table and handed me the joint.

I read somewhere that a lie is like murder. The liar murders truth. I've heard of wasted lies—lies that aren't told for any specific purpose. I didn't know what kind of lie I'd told. It blew out of me like a geyser, and I couldn't put it away.

I took one more hit off that bone, and then I shook a pointed finger down at that big, black Caddy parked out front, smiled my best dope-notion smile, and reached for my voice.

"I'm throwing a dinner party for the Caddy."

15

I HAD A pot full of gravy, and my lasagna filling chilling. I had to brown the chicken and thaw a quart of my frozen marinara for the cacciatore, and then put the big pot on to boil the lasagna noodles. The cripple came in and watched me. I gave my Yankee cup a rest—didn't want to get sloshed and not enjoy my dinner.

While the chicken browned and the noodle water heated up, I talked about doing things like driving to Disney World in the Caddy.

"I know people along the way, fun people who will take us in. I know a couple in Virginia just outside of DC, and I have a friend who lives on the Outer Banks in Duck, North Carolina."

"That's out of the way."

"Mr. Cheer."

The phone rang. It was Cooper. Turned out he kept all the numbers of his crew in case of emergency, and my number was for Ronny. "I'm drinking at Tessinger's, drinking liquor. Get Hopkins."

After Ronny hung up, I got the lowdown.

"He left the beach right after my spill. He didn't want his wife to know he cut out early to go to a bar."

"He never goes to bars?"

"He said going to a bar before he went home to her, and the kids would finish it. His words—finish it. He didn't make any sense. Anyway, he wants us to pick up him and his bicycle."

"His bicycle?"

"He won't drive drunk. Not even his bicycle. He remembered your car. My bike will tuck into Jimmy's car he said."

"Why the hell won't he ride a bike drunk?"

"He won't ride a bike drunk; he won't stand on a sidewalk with a beer. It's a holiday town, but Cooper's stuck in a permanent work cubicle."

"Well, you can't drive my car with that foot and with all of your drinking."

"I can manage."

"No way. Not my Caddy."

I turned off the water and my sauce and picked up my car keys. Now the noodles were going to stick together. I went back, got each one, and laid them side by side on wax paper. When we left, I went down the stairs first and let Ronny lean on me as he hopped.

After three step hops he muttered, "This is bullshit," and started walking on his heel. On the way to the car, he discovered he could put his weight on the outside of his foot instead of walking like Long John Silver. What an act. All for a damn splinter. Marijuana, straight vodka, and Novocain shots should have been enough to mask a shattered tibia.

"We have a half hour to get there, find Cooper, and take him and his bicycle home. My sauce is at risk."

I got excited just thinking about opening the Caddy's door. "Brother-be-Jesus I'm behind her wheel." I guided that car with one hand—not a bit of steering. I blew the horn driving along Ocean Ave. People walking on the boardwalk started to wave and call to us. I pulled over a little, stopped dead in the street, put both hands over my head, and shook them like FDR in newsreels. All we needed was tickertape.

Tessinger's is a tavern on Brady just off F Street that caters mostly to locals. It has fresh squeezed screwdrivers, bartenders with black bow ties, and a men's room that reminds me of Mafia movies.

I double parked outside Tessinger's.

"Go get him."

Ronny took two steps to Tessinger's door. It was more than a couple of minutes until they came out.

"My God," Cooper said, "what is this?"

"Service. You had to have a drink, didn't you? While I'm out here waiting for a ticket."

"I just finished Cooper's."

Two guys trying to get out of Tessinger's had to wait for Cooper to load his bike. He had it chained to the wrought iron railing by the entrance and couldn't work the combination on the bike lock.

"He's holding us up," Ronny pointed a thumb at Cooper.

"We can wait." Combined they would have made one and a quarter of Cooper.

Cooper bumbled the bike in the back and climbed in with it. I turned around. "I'll make you some coffee and then you can ride home from my place."

He grunted, "Fine with me."

At home, I checked my noodles, got the filling out of the fridge, and stirred my sauce. I gave Cooper his coffee.

"I hope you appreciate this, Cooper," Ronny said.

Cooper didn't answer.

Ronny started laughing. "How'd you like the door-to-door service?"

Still, not a peep. I didn't mind. At least Cooper managed to break up the sniping between my hobbled guest and me, but he had a bad case of the stares. He looked up from his imaginary bug race on the balcony, sized me up and down—maybe he was out of focus—and spoke up.

"What's the smell?"

"What's wrong, you aren't in Jersey? That's tomato gravy. In a while, it'll be lasagna. You'll taste the smell."

"I don't know." Cooper lifted one foot and started to knock flaking paint off the top of the balcony railing with his sneaker. He knocked off big chips, then sat up and leaned over to watch them helicopter to the ground. I poked his shoulder.

"How about the coffee? Drink up."

He kept right on scraping and watching. I should have given him a wire brush and let him do the whole damn railing. Then I realized something.

"Excuse me. I know your last name, but I forgot your first. We have Ron, Jimmy, and—"

"Sam."

"Sam. Why don't you drink your coffee, Sam?"

Cooper's foot flopped off the railing. He folded his hands and leaned forward, his head hanging down at the bug races again. "I'm drunk now. I've been drinking for hours."

Ronny got up to go to the bathroom. Cooper watched him walk away and sipped his coffee. I motioned inside. "Ronny had quite a fall."

"He did."

"He'll be back. You're a Sunday drinker, aren't you, Sam? Like a Sunday driver."

"Do you live here?" Cooper raised his head and looked around. I had hope.

"I sure do."

He looked over his shoulder, inside the sliding door, but only for a second. Then his head slumped down, and he started to drip-spit on the balcony. Saliva stretched down from his lips.

"What are doing, Cooper?" He ignored me. The next drip's string broke. He produced another. "How about spitting over the edge?"

A little puddle formed right in front of him. When I saw Ronny open the bathroom door, I went inside.

"Cooper's making spit puddles out there."

Ronny looked out and then waved for me to follow him into the kitchen. On the way I put on the Rascal's *Time Peace*—their greatest hits. Ronny laughed.

"What the hell? Is he spitting coffee?"

"He's spitting spit. Do you know his wife's number? Let her take him home so he spits on his own balcony."

"That's the real problem, his wife."

"I see. You don't want to piss him off, do you?"

"Why don't you go out there and talk to him?"

"You want me as counselor or cook?"

I got a Coke out of the fridge, some ice, a glass, and poured in the soda. It fizzed to the top and bubbled down. I turned to the stove and my dinner.

"Okay, okay." Ronny went out on the balcony with Cooper, and the next thing I heard was, "Cooper, for God's sake!"

Copper had his face in his hands. Ronny stood over him for a minute, patted him on the shoulder, and then came back inside and started looking through my records. I had a stack on the spindle, and he started replacing some of them.

"Don't you dare take off *Time Peace*."

I built my lasagna, put it in the oven, and went back out to the balcony. Cooper had stopped spitting, and he looked in control of himself. He turned to me. I must have had a *What's My Line?* expression on my face, because out of nowhere came, "Why did you and your wife split up, Jimmy?"

"That was a long time ago. A long time ago and besides, personal business is not a topic for a dinner party."

"Okay." He proceeded to open up about wifey and the marriage. It wasn't a unique story. I met Denise, a nice person. Cooper, too, I suppose—just headed in different directions.

"I'm happy with teaching, coaching, and guarding. She says she's stuck with the kids at home all day all year."

Ronny rescued me. He came out, grabbed Cooper's arm, and took him into the kitchen. I watched him show Cooper the lasagna in the oven. I had a few puffs on a cigar. The smoke hung thick in the humidity. Before I went back inside, I splashed Cooper's spit puddle off the balcony with my Coke.

The AC felt good. "That evening air's a little heavy outside, Sam. And that southeast breeze quit."

Ronny opened the refrigerator door and took out the antipasto. "See this? Nice, healthy food."

Cooper picked up an artichoke heart and stared at it. "What is this?"

"A diseased tomato." Ronny looked at me. "Fucking hopeless."

Cooper ignored him and went into the bathroom.

I shook my head at Ronny. "Big Sam's got problems."

Ronny picked up the phone and hit some numbers.

"Who are you calling?"

He looked at me as if I'd asked him for his bank account number. Then I saw an Estel's matchbook on the table next to the phone. He waved for me to go away. I did. Right to the extension in my room.

There was nobody on the line, but there were sounds in the background. Then Robin picked up.

"Hello."

"This is a voice from your past."

"Hello, Ron," her tone dropped. "Ron?"

"I would very much like you to come to dinner this evening at Jimmy's. Very informal, nobody's dressing up. It'll only take you forty-five minutes to get down."

She didn't say anything right away, and he jumped in.

"I need it as a favor. It's Jimmy—his cancer's back. He's down in the dumps and bought a Caddy to cheer himself up. I think I'm asking you very hard."

He didn't waste an angle. I hung up and went back to the kitchen. He had the stereo turned down so he could hear his call.

"I'll be on the boardwalk there. You'll recognize me. I'll be the guy standing on one good leg. Ah, I took a header on the boards. A splinter the width of five pencils went through the ball of my foot. You should have heard Casivette…"

A fisherman's tale—everything grew. I hung up and went back to the living room. Ronny hung up. I waited for him to say something. "So?"

"She's coming."

That stoked me. I forgot about him using my lie. Robin would be here. I could show off the car, the dinner. I realized in that same moment that Cooper should stick around.

"Sam, you're staying for dinner. Make you feel better. So Ronny—you, me, Cooper, Robin. Who else can you call? Make it an Inlet affair. Call Vinny and Harris. Get Annie up here. There's plenty."

I had the fresh prosciutto dolce, capicola, and salami on the antipasto; I had fresh bread; I had the chicken browned along with my marinara sauce, and fresh mozzarella for cacciatore.

Not too many people give a good dinner party. It's a lost art. Start with the host or hostess. Some try to organize things as if the party's a two-minute drill. Everybody's here—cocktails. Slug down half a drink—hors d'oeuvres appear. Then time for a cigarette and boom, out comes dinner. By the time dessert and coffee are served, everybody feels like a restaurant's first seating on

Mother's Day. People don't know whether to leave or stand around. What's next, home movies?

The Italians had the right idea. You sat down, had some wine, smoked, talked, and all the time, food appeared, one course after the other. Nobody rushed or wondered what the hell to do.

That's what I planned; except I didn't have a table big enough to seat everyone. I did, but it had my radio equipment all over it. It had to be buffet style. Surprises are nice at a dinner party. I thought of one, got on the phone, and made a call to an old friend.

Ronny called Vinny while I got out bottles of Chianti.

"Never mind that, it's fine. I need you and a date for an off-the-cuff dinner party at Jimmy's. How about it? Lasagna, antipasto, the whole bit."

"Cacciatore."

"Jimmy says cacciatore, too." Ronny talked some more on the phone, hung up, and stood next to me at the stove. "Okay. He needs to find a date. Half an hour."

"That makes six. How many should we shoot for?"

"We could call Denise and watch the fun."

"No. And Annie won't come alone. What about Harris?" I knew before I finished the thought. He'd feel out of place. I opened the oven and checked the lasagna. It bubbled in its big, clear baking dish, full to the edges. "Six is fine."

"Looks like enough for sixty. Here comes Cooper. I'm using the shower."

"Need a baggie for your sock?"

"I'll stick it out the curtain." Ronny started another screwdriver.

Cooper came alongside me, got himself another coffee, and leaned against the wall. My marinara sauce melted down in its pot. I threw my sautéed onions and peppers into the chicken pan and poured in some wine to deglaze it.

"Hopkins, this guy's unbelievable. I always thought he was just a rummy."

"Jimmy's this town's local color. And his hearing's just fine."

I smiled at Cooper. "Sam. I ever tell you this dream I have? I'm a knight, or a prince, or something like that. I'm sent out to kill this big thing, a monster. I kill it, and people circle around, staring at it. Then they walk away, and there's disappointment in their faces. Know why?" I used the Italian bread for the monster and a knife for my sword.

"No."

"I took a big part of their world from them, the one thing they could count on to blame and complain about. Without it, they would have to look to other things—maybe themselves. Except my dream's backwards," I smiled. "I'm the loaf."

I finished arranging the cold cuts. I made garlic butter for the bread. The cacciatore simmered away, and the lasagna would be out soon and cooling.

Ronny got out of the bathroom. He left it a steamy mess—water all over the bathmat and floor. I got my beard and mustache trimmer from under the sink and trimmed up my mustache. I gave it more of an Ernest Hemingway look than a Hulk Hogan—I cut those long tails at the corners of the mouth. I trimmed up my hair a little around the ears, and then I had a nice, careful shave.

I got dressed and went into the kitchen. Two minutes later Vinny and his date stormed up the stairs.

"Oh, my God," Vinny waved a hand under his nostrils. He came straight for the kitchen, leaned over the stove, and circled a cupped hand toward his face. His date stood at the top of the stairs, her hands at her sides, one leg turned and out in front. She looked around at the fun house.

I walked over to her. "Welcome." I never extend a hand first to a woman. "I'm Jimmy. And you are?"

"Marsha."

Her eyes smiled. I don't know where Vinny finds them. She looked like she'd stepped off a *Cosmo* cover. I led her over to the couch and saw to it that she had a cocktail—half a glass of wine. Then I headed out to the balcony for a break. Ronny and Cooper came along.

"It's cooler out here," Cooper said. "With the oven cranking, cooler outside than in."

"You're getting your senses back, Cooper."

"Watching for her?" I said to Ronny.

"Denise? You didn't call Denise, did you?"

"He didn't mean Denise, Cooper. Give her a rest. Let the rest of us drink and eat in peace."

"I'm blowing off steam. That's all I'm doing. How about Vinny's date?"

"Quite a girl."

"Yeah," Ronny snickered, "he left her at the steps and hit the kitchen. Must be their second date. A first date he'd be glued to the whole time."

We all went back in and sat. Vinny had a beer, and he stood in front of us as if we were playing charades after Marsha went to the bathroom.

"I know her sister. Back home my friend owns a laundry. He set me up with the sister. Me an' her had sex in a back room in a big canvas cart filled with silk sheets. The sister left, and I fell asleep. Next morning the open-up lady comes in and sees my arman' leg stickin' out the cart. She screams, I sit up and scream, and she screams more."

The doorbell rang. I came around the corner from the kitchen and looked at Ronny. Nobody ever rings my doorbell—they just come up.

"Shit, how'd I miss her? I told her I'd meet her on the boardwalk."

"Meet her at the door."

The bell rang again.

"I'll answer it," Cooper said. Ronny waited at the top of the stairs for Robin.

I came out with a glass of Chianti for her. "Ron tells me you like a good glass of wine. Enjoy."

She leaned forward and kissed me on the cheek as natural as could be. She poked Ronny's leg with a finger.

"Is this your excuse for not coming up to the boardwalk?"

He laughed, looking down at his foot. "There goes the summer."

She came around in front of him. "It's a cleaned puncture wound. That'll heal from the inside out. Didn't anyone ever tell you saltwater helps things heal?"

"I've heard that. I've also heard the water's full of bacteria."

"You have to keep cheerful." Then she looked at me. "Have to be positive."

"Absolutely." What the hell else could I say?

I got the antipasto circulating, and then put it on the little table in the kitchen along with my favorite cocktail napkins. The napkins read *I am not a fast bartender. I am not a slow bartender. I am a half-fast bartender. What's yours?* I put out plates with cocktail forks—fancy salad forks—I have a set of eight.

With my big lie about the cancer, for a few hours on that evening back in June, I got that starting all over sensation.

One thing about living in a small town that just happens to have an ocean on its eastern border—every summer brings something new. Some locals get caught up. They figure summer's just around the corner. Before they know it, they're stuck. Old timers have a name for locals who get stuck in summer 365 days a year—clam diggers.

I detected the aroma of marijuana. Mr. Hopkins had a bone going, and just then, the doorbell rang—twice in one evening.

This time it had to be my buddy Oscar with his accordion. A long- time Belmar boy, he'd played that squeezebox since we were in elementary school together. He did small gatherings and belonged to the local Chamber of Commerce. All decked out in his black tux with red tie and cummerbund, at the top of the stairs he ran up and down the scale a few times before he launched into "Lady of Spain."

Vinny held his sides, laughing. He grabbed Marsha and started twirling her. Ronny took hold of Robin, stood on one leg, and spun her a few times. I conducted Oscar with a wooden spoon. Ronny held the bone in front of Oscar's mouth. He toked and didn't miss a riff.

After "Lady of Spain," I announced, "An old acquaintance, Mr. Oscar Kaplan. He will be here for two hours to entertain us."

Oscar played a tarantella or three and then closed the dancing portion of his program with "Na Na Hey Hey Kiss Him Goodbye." He had everybody up and jiving. I even had a turn with Robin. I did damn well for an old clam digger.

"Jimmy, you're beautiful," Vinny said.

I blew him a kiss. Robin wanted to help me serve.

"He won't let you," Ronny said.

I let her. Even Oscar had to marvel at the food coming out of that little kitchen. I had no room to seat everyone, so I put everything out at once. When the last platter was out, and more bottles of Chianti opened, I received a round of applause. I held up my hands, swept a glass of wine off the counter, and waved good-bye as if everybody had gotten on a bus. Then I went into my room and stretched out on my bed for a rest.

Between Oscar's selections, I heard Ronny say, "He's resting and digesting. Jimmy tastes as he cooks."

"All good cooks do," Robin said.

Plates being stacked woke me up. Silverware rattled. Oscar started up the digestion music, calm and melodious. Listening, I drifted into my mural. Alice painted a mural on the east wall of my bedroom a few years back. It's where a window with a view of the ocean would be if it weren't for the apartment between mine and the beach. She knew I liked to have the ocean nearby, so she made it look as close as she could to the real thing. She skipped Ocean Ave and the boardwalk and went right to the beach. Everything's seen from above— not too high, but high enough to get a better than stand-up view of the umbrellas, the people swimming, walking the shoreline, lying out.

The day she finished it, I told her, "It makes me feel like I'm sleeping on a picture postcard. I can lie in bed, look at it, and feel the sun hot against the back of my neck and shoulders, a good breeze blowing, cooling my face, kicking up a big shore break when the tide's full and high."

A little while later, after Oscar closed with "We've Only Just Begun." Ronny came in. He sat down on my bed.

"Well, we're all stuffed. The kitchen's a nightmare. The girls cleaned up a little, put away the leftovers. Robin, anyway. You got the stares, buddy. Looking at your mural?"

"Who the hell requested, "We've Only Just Begun?""

"Vinny. I was wrong. It's his first date with Marsha. You know what I think is boss about it? Your mural? I like the viewpoint. It's like being up on the stand, above everybody, in control. All those people in the water—they'd be mine. You having spumoni? You've never passed it up."

Outside in the living room I heard laughing, calling out for song requests.

"Oscar's running the turn table. The Chianti's flowing," Ronny stood up. "It's a hell of a party, Jimmy. Don't miss any more of it."

"You're right. Hosts can't disappear."

I threw my door open. The only person I saw at first was Oscar. He stood over the sink, hands lost in the suds.

"I knew you were coming back out, so I saved you a big piece of spumoni," he nodded down at a plate on the drain board.

"Where is everybody?"

"Two on the balcony," he turned around, his hands out of the water. "Two on the couch," he whispered and pointed his chin.

The balcony slider opened. Its rubber stop banged with a thud. Cooper roared in, Ronny on his heels.

"It hasn't been my day. When I saw her leaning toward you the way someone does when she's listening to every word that corked it."

Vinny and Marsha's heads popped above the couch.

"There's Jimmy," Cooper pointed. "You better see to his spumoni."

"Where's Robin?" I held out my hands.

Oscar dried his hands. "The pretty nurse went for some fresh air," he swiveled his head at Cooper and Ronny. "I was just leaving."

I gave him a nice tip. "Extra for the dishes."

He grabbed his instrument and left like he'd spotted accordion Vandals.

"Have a seat, Hoppy," Vinny stood up.

Ronny ignored him, went out on the balcony, and called, "Robin!" He held the railing with both hands, leaned over and looked down. I got out there and was about to tell him to shut the hell up when I heard Robin's voice underneath the balcony. I went down my stairs and found her on the top step of my little porch.

"What's going on?"

"I've been sitting here, waiting for the foolishness to stop. Those two, Ronny and Sam. All I did was listen to Sam," she threw up both hands.

"Come up with me."

We got upstairs. I called everybody into the living room. I sat them all down. That lasted three seconds for Cooper and Ronny. They got up and paced on either side of the couch. I felt like Mr. Rogers in front of a small group of incorrigibles—not including Robin.

"What gives?"

"It's nothing," Ronny said.

"He thought his girl paid me too much attention. She was just trying to help. I'm not thinking about your girl, asshole."

"Cooper's still on his roller coaster."

"Ronny, we were talking."

"He wants to be able to find answers the way he diagrams football plays. Hey, Cooper. Give your kid a call at least. I promise you'll feel better—"

Robin looked up at him, "Ron."

"It was just a suggestion."

"*Kids.* We have two. How the hell can you promise anything, Hopkins?" He wasn't loud. His voice shook, and he looked at the floor. "That's a good one, coming from you. Promise, my ass. What can I do that I haven't done already? I've done the best I can. Isn't there something in some promise about that? About doing your best and having things work out?"

"You think your kids are starting to wonder where you are, Cooper?"

I could see Cooper focus on Ronny. I thought shit; he is *way* too big to get pissed.

"Look, you two," Robin stood up, "this world's throw away happy. You have to keep everything you learn, and that means everyone you ever love, inside of you. You can't afford to let a single one of them get away. Sam, go home to Denise. Jimmy, with me out on the balcony."

She took my arm, walked me outside, and closed the slider. The questions flew out of her mouth, all of them medical, too technical, and full of terms I didn't remember.

"Am I making sense? You haven't even nodded."

"I don't know how to answer you. None of this you're asking is going to help me. I'm too stubborn to listen."

"You won't let anybody ask questions. You'll put down your voice and stare. Is that what you're telling me?"

"I'm good for now. I'll see the oncologist again soon. Go see Ronny. Calm him down."

She looked at me and smiled. "Promise to keep positive."

I nodded. I felt like shit.

"Dinner was fabulous."

"Thank you," I stood up.

I followed her inside. I didn't see Cooper anywhere, and nothing was broken. Vinny and Marsha were on the couch. They both looked at me like what time does the balloon go up? More thanks as they left. Their time making out on the couch hadn't rustled one hair on Marsha's head out of place.

Ronny smiled at Robin. He held a hand out to her. "Thanks for Cooper. You and Jimmy have the talk?" Robin took his hand and they embraced. She came just to his chest.

"We did." She turned her head, maybe listening to his heart. They came apart, and he hopped down the steps behind her. I sat on the couch and turned on the TV.

I was half-asleep when Ronny came back up.

"Not up for driving me to Commodore, are you?"

"Not even half-way."

"Robin said to say thanks again."

"Did she say anything else? About you two?"

"What do you mean?"

"Did she say anything about getting together again?"

"Something about we'll have other times."

"What did you say?" I rolled my hand.

"How about tomorrow."

I don't know if I was happy and hopeful for him or for me. All I knew was I'd see her again.

"We'll have a bone on the balcony. I have one rolled."

"Only if you tell me what you told Robin. What exactly did the doctor say?"

"I'll be right back. The bone's in my room." I took my voice with me and left it on my nightstand. I put on *Time Out for Smokey Robinson and the Miracles*, and we went out on the balcony and smoked. We watched the traffic pass, the drunks coming out of the dance bar trying to remember where they had parked their cars. Out on the water, the party boats had a meeting. A breeze came up and rolled the mist like cotton candy past the streetlights and along the blacktop. No sooner did Ronny have his foot propped than the phone rang.

I didn't move. At first, he wasn't going to answer it, but he did.

"Hello. I've been here. Well, you know how Sundays are—Mondays."

I went inside. I thought it had to be Peggy when he launched into his tale of woe. He kept this version short. I don't know what she said after he finished, but it dragged on and on.

"Jimmy's been seeing to my needs."

"You let in a big, green fly," I mouthed.

I wish I could have heard Peggy's explanation of what she would do that I wouldn't. I laughed thinking about that.

"That sounds interesting. You should see Jimmy's new Caddy."

The Caddy. I never did show it to Robin. I mouthed, "Tell her not to call here again. Ever."

He wouldn't hand me the phone. "Yeah. Peggy? Look, Peggy, I'm beat." He held the receiver out and looked at it. "Good night, Peggy." He tried to hang up but missed the cradle. The receiver dropped and yo-yoed. "I'm all in." He hung up, went into his room, and shut the door.

I went down and locked the front door. The phone was one thing—I didn't want any surprise visits. Back in the kitchen, I saw the remains of my spumoni. Finished melting, it had spilled over the plate's edge onto the drain board. Multi-colored trails ran down into the sink.

I mouthed, "Why the hell didn't he say goodbye to that woman?"

I started cleaning up the mess. A wine glass slipped out of my hand into the suds left in the sink and broke. I felt around for shards, waiting for that stab of pain. I parted the suds with the spray hose to find all the pieces. After that, I called it quits.

16

WATCHING TUESDAY MORNING TV, Ronny told me, "I have to go downtown to where Casivette eats breakfast and talk to him. My foot feels like somebody stuck an air needle in and pumped it full."

"Good. We'll both go. Let somebody cook for me."

I went in my room for my wallet and keys, and when I came out, Ronny had switched the channel to cable TV news.

"What's this?" I pointed at the set.

"I'm waiting for the weather."

"Look out the window. What happened to *The Little Rascals?*"

"I've seen that one."

I flipped it back. "We've all seen all of them. It's Mister Hood's birthday party."

"Where they give him a frog, a cat, and a duck and then take them back."

"I love it when Mr. Hood says all he had to eat today was a lettuce sandwich on gluten bread. He doesn't get a crumb. His soup gets cold, the kids devour his chicken, and Percy steals the last piece of birthday cake."

"Are you fucking Siskel or Ebert?"

"Neither. There's you yesterday," I laughed when Mr. Hood whined.

"The way you watch this shit you'd think it was the seventh game of the World Series."

"I'm hungry. Casivette eats at White's, doesn't he?"

"To get the discount like everybody else."

White's is the mayor's place, and all borough employees get a 10% discount.

"Who's driving? What discount do they give to former employees?"

"They let you count your change."

"You drive." In the bright morning sun coming off the water and beach, she looked blacker than ever. "Let's go topless."

Ronny drove left footed. He stuck his right over the transmission hump. It took some getting used to. The first time he hit those power brakes, I thought we were both going through the windshield.

"Clutch pressure," was his excuse.

"At least there's no traffic. Just a straight shot down Ocean and then right on Monmouth."

When we passed the Commodore, I smiled, "How's your room?"

"For what they charge it's not too good."

Ronny parallel parked the Caddy. I got a little morning sun, some color on my face while he managed that.

Inside White's, Casivette and a few of the elite guards gobbled their breakfasts. They sat at the counter, Casivette in the middle. He shoveled eggs onto his fork with a piece of toast and didn't notice us. Ronny and I got a booth just behind him. The girl came by to drop off the menus. Ronny ordered two coffees.

When I looked up from the menu, I spotted familiar faces at tables toward the back of White's. Besides the guards, there were some DPW people eating, too. They were all done—they had to be at work by 8:00. I recognized some of the regulars, the year-round employees.

When the borough boys got up to leave, I saw Denny. He came over and put a hand on my shoulder. "Jimmy Hanlon. Jimmy O'Hanlon O' Jimmy. How are you? Good to see you."

"Sullivan—brush." I stood up and gave him a hug. Denny still drove the brush truck in summer. From my balcony I'd see him ride by every so often in his truck and wave. He sent me a nice card and came to see me in the hospital after my laryngectomy. "Always good to see you, my friend."

Casivette heard my voice popping, turned around and saw us.

"Can you walk?" He looked at Ronny.

"I can walk." He got up and walked over to him. "I want to talk to you about work."

"Talk." The cheap bastard hunted through change for a tip.

"Look, I still want to work through the Fourth."

Casivette pointed down at the foot. "How is it? You need today off? Who's off today on your crew?"

"Nobody."

"Now you are. That was easy. I'm not putting you on comp for one day. It takes me a whole night to do the paperwork."

I had an inkling Ronny was going to ask about after the Fourth, but he didn't.

"I'll be at work tomorrow."

"So will I. Early. You need to be able to do your job."

After Casivette and his minions left, Ronny said, "I know what Casivette meant by that early business. He's going to check my walk."

"He doesn't want any limp. People on the beach would wonder."

"If a job came up, I'd be fine. I have no doubts. Like you said, people wonder. They imagine the worst. They also look at an eighteen-year-old who weighs one-sixty and then picture Uncle Louie, all two-eighty of him, floundering around out there. I've told you a hundred times. It's about watching, anticipating, and knowing the water."

We finished breakfast. With Ronny's day off and our bellies full, we did some cruising. We drove past places I hadn't seen in almost a year. We passed the old Carlton Hotel annex. They've made some improvements to it. The annex, known as the Carlton Junior, is a dump. Rooms so small you couldn't pass out in them sideways.

Ronny said, "I almost forgot. I have a date, a dinner date, with Robin in the Highlands. She had to go home to Paterson. She wants to meet me at the Clam House at 6:00."

"News to me."

"I told you last night. Robin asked what time?"

I remembered. When I got to my building, I pulled up and let the Caddy run. "Hell, take my car. Enjoy your dinner. Stay out of the Captain's Room today." I got out and watched him scoot across the seat. "Be good to Robin," I patted the Caddy, "and to her, too."

"Thanks Jimmy. It's the Engine Room." He gunned the Caddy and raced down to the stop sign.

I spent the day chatting—Annie, Mr. Lipp at J's. I watched a little TV. I found a good movie—Humphrey Bogart, Lauren Bacall and Walter Brennan in *To Have and Have Not*. Brennan got that limp he used for *The Real McCoys* by putting a stone in one shoe. Acting's a lie without complications.

For me it had been a mild, June day. It hung around, rolled right into the evening, and never thought about changing for dinner. I fell asleep on my balcony. Long after dark, a car horn came to me from a distance, waking me. It turned a corner, moved closer until it blew like hell right under my feet. Ronny climbed out of my Caddy, and I waved him up to the balcony to hear about his date.

17

DRESSED BY FIVE with a full tank of gas and a wad of bills in his pocket, Ronny put the top down, found his radio station, and pulled from a parking spot outside the Commodore. He and Robin agreed on the Highlands because of its proximity and seafood restaurants. He drove the ocean route all the way up to catch the sights from a drop top.

Riding over the Inlet Bridge, he twisted off the screw cap on a Bud. Traffic was heavy in places, but he was early. Once he rounded the lake in Bradley and turned into Asbury, the traffic thinned. He drove past the old Berkley Carteret. It looked like it wanted to pull its shades down and rest.

Around the lake into Deal. What a contrast. Houses so big and fine. Cops everywhere--he saw three sitting on side streets. They gave the Caddy the eye. The road narrowed, twisting through Monmouth Beach, alongside the sea wall, and then over the bridge into the Highlands. At a light a '62 Falcon all jazzed up idled next to a Mercedes-Benz 560sl.

The Clam House sat right on the water at the Navesink's mouth. The lot was half-full. He didn't see Robin's car in the parking lot. Inside he gave his name to the maître d' and walked into the lounge. Two waitresses leaned against the bar. He sat at a table. The younger one with long blond hair came over.

"Hi."

"Good evening. I'll have a dry vodka martini, up, with an olive."

She looked a little like Sally Field in her Smokey and the Bandit days. He watched her standing at the service bar waiting for his martini. She glanced at him, smiling.

He figured a two-martini limit. He polished off number two when the ship wheel clock's hands formed a straight line at six.

The cocktail waitress came to his table. Bending, she placed thumb and forefinger under the rim of his martini glass and whisked it onto her tray.

"Care for another?"

"Not just now."

She emptied his ashtray into hers. "I wouldn't leave you waiting in a lounge by yourself."

He ordered number three just as the maître d' came into the lounge.

"Do you care to be seated for your six o'clock reservation?"

"I'm an incomplete party."

The second time the maître d' asked, he added, "We're getting busy, sir."

The third time he asked, Ronny whispered, "Not yet, douchebag." After the maître d' told him that he would have to leave, Ronny smiled up at him, "Did you know your ears are full of twisty hair?"

Outside he walked down the parking lot closer to the river bridge. The water ran fast there. He lit a cigarette and watched it. All that water squeezed tight by the river and ocean currents took the easiest path along the surface, glass-smooth, past pilings roped together where the mirror came apart and the current showed in straight, quick lines.

A car horn damn near blew him into the river.

"Catching dinner?"

He pointed at his wrist. "If I were your patient, I'd be dead by now."

She stared at him for a few seconds and then pulled into a parking space. She didn't get out of the car or turn it off. He walked over, knelt, and folded his arms on her door.

"I'm sorry. It wasn't the right thing to say. Let's start over."

He went around to the passenger door and got in. She had both hands on the steering wheel. He put a hand into his pants pocket, pulled out an imaginary coin, and dropped it into a pay phone. Reciting her number, he pushed buttons in the air.

He kept a fist next to his ear. "At least answer it. It's ringing off the hook."

Her lips pinched together, and she smiled, picked up a receiver off the wheel, and held it to her cheek. "Hello."

"Hello. Look, about tonight." He waited. It was like an actual phone call. He didn't know what the hell to say. "Instead of six, let's say seven-thirty. Ah, instead of the Clam House, let's make it Garner's in Sea Bright."

"Sounds good." She put her receiver back on the wheel. Still smiling, "You can hang up now."

She followed the Caddy. He kept down the speed and she stuck tight on his fins. They were seated right away at Garner's. Robin ran a finger around the rim of the water glass making it sing.

He ordered. "Steamers, a big bucket of them. Some people call them pisser clams. The foot sticks out—some people call it the neck—and you need to peel the skin off before you eat the clam."

"I've never eaten them."

"I'll teach you."

They decided on a bottle of chardonnay.

"You're a wonderful girl," he laughed when she got a steamer that was all sand and spit it out in her napkin.

They both ordered lobster, so they got the bit with the plastic bibs. Ronny tore that crustacean apart. Butter dripped; lobster guts flecked the white tablecloth. All through the lobsters, an old couple in pastels talked at the next table about which was worse for you, salt, or cholesterol.

Ronny drank a beer for dessert. Robin sipped Grand Marnier. He looked out Garner's front window at all the brake lights playing stop and go after Robin said, "What are we going to do about Jimmy's cancer?"

"What can we do?"

Technical talk. Treatment options. He nodded, lit a cigarette looking at the bill. The whole time Robin spoke, he remembered once being the guest of a girl at Sea Bright Beach club across the street. The girl showed him how easy it was to sneak onto the beach from the parking lot. All you had to do was hop the three-foot parking lot fence without the gate attendant, who left work at five, spotting you.

Outside Garner's the streetlights had just come on.

"Let's go see the ocean."

He took her hand, walked her to the fence, and they climbed over it. On the lot's south side, ten feet of concrete ran east west as reinforcement, and below that was the sand. The air felt good, the breaking waves a tonic. He walked on the outside of his foot as if he was about to kick soccer style. Robin kept looking down, shaking her head.

"Are we supposed to be here?"

"The beach manager is my cousin's uncle."

"Which makes him—"

"Not around right now."

They sat with their backs against the guard storage locker facing the water. At high tide, the beach was only twenty yards wide—nothing like Belmar. Ronny stood and opened the locker.

"I can't believe they don't lock this. Just for the hell of it. I want to check what kind of lifesaving apparatus they use here in Sea Bright."

"Somebody is going to see you."

"All their stuff is wedged into one corner. Their line's all sandy. Wonder if they had a job today. I don't see a daily log."

"For God's sake get down," she laughed. "Is this where they keep the hostages?" She stood next to him to investigate the locker, and he let go of the hatch. People passing by in headlights on the sidewalk looked when it banged shut.

"They can't see you."

"Oh my God," she hissed.

"They figure we belong here."

He sat against her, brushed back her hair, and waited. When she didn't look away, he kissed her. He put his whole day into that kiss. She pulled away, smiling, "That was nice."

"You know the reason most cops check the beach at night? They're hoping to catch some flounder. That's two people making love on the beach. They give the lucky couple time for things to get started. Then they bring a spot to bear on what's bare. They've caught some flounder."

Robin laughed, "That's ridiculous."

"On a beach like Sea Bright, though, the couple has a chance. It's hidden from the street by the clubhouse."

She laughed with her eyes.

"Let's see if we get caught."

"That's your lobster talking," she leaned over and kissed him on the cheek.

"Let's stay here in damp sand with no blanket, no sense, and no chance of getting away if we get caught."

She smiled down at the sand.

"Would you buy a used car from me if I hummed an old Beach Boys tune?"

They kissed. This time she didn't pull away. She started to laugh, but he made a noise in his throat to shush her. Voices and traffic sounds mixed with the waves. She turned, put her arms around him, and let herself fall to the sand. He opened his eyes and watched her face move back and forth. Beyond her the water out past the breakers was a black mirror holding long tails of light rippling toward them from big boats anchored far offshore. He closed his eyes, pulled her shirt out from her jeans, and ran his hand underneath.

She broke away from him. "Enough." She propped herself up on an elbow and looked at him.

He looked back at her. "What?"

She didn't say anything. She dropped her eyes.

"Hey, why pull me down?" he laughed. "Why follow a gimp all the way here?"

"I suppose I asked for that. You fooled me. It surprised me. Not here, not now. Don't think it hasn't been on my mind, isn't on my mind. My God," she smiled up at the sky.

At that point, there were no words in him. Her words meant nothing.

On the sidewalk, she thanked him for dinner. He walked her to her car, watched its taillights ride north and turn left to cross over Highlands Bridge. It occurred to him that it would have been a hell of a lot quicker to take the ocean route through the Highlands instead of going through Red Bank traffic to hit the Parkway.

18

ROBIN AND I hit the beach so early we beat the cleaning crew Wednesday—a clear sky over a calm ocean. Blinking back the low sunlight, we shared the morning quiet with a couple of large coffees and yesterday's *Asbury Park Press* from J's. We were down even before Mr. Casivette, who came to the beach to see if a certain guard showed any visible sign of physical injury. He shouldn't have bothered. Robin gave Ronny a gross of flesh-colored bandages for his foot. Other than two fingers on his big toe that were wrapped around from underneath, there was nothing noticeable.

"Not even going to end up with a white spot to ruin his foot tan he told me."

Robin put down her section of the *Press*. "Ronny told me you've had a recurrence." She sounded as if she'd just read it.

I managed a nod, and Robin talked about scopes, options, and not smoking. I picked up sections of the *Press* I'd already read, pretending to listen. What the hell could I say?

"I'm thinking about my options," I told her. I was. Disney World in any case.

In Monterey, California, I tended bar full time—a day shift in a dinner and jazz venue. Not many people came to lunch or sat in the bar. I needed the work, though, so I took the job.

I did have one regular. He never ate except for the free pretzels on the bar. He drank what he called half-and-half: scotch, cream, no ice. He had stomach cancer. He never talked about it except for once when he told me why he had an unusual drink choice.

Instead, we talked fighters. He knew a ton about the lighter weight classes. I believe he might have been a fighter at one time. He claimed these guys today don't stand on their toes. They fight flat-footed. He threw out names and dates. So and so could punch; that guy was strictly a bleeder. Guys I never

123

heard of. The words *the Garden*, as in Madison Square Garden, were in every other sentence. He always came in grumpy, but he didn't leave that way most of the time. "See you tomorrow," he would always say when he left. You know how it ended.

I promised Robin I'd check with my oncologist about options soon, and that I'd give up smoking cigars and cigarettes—I'd just puff.

"Not marijuana. I can't cook without tasting, and I taste best wasted."

She laughed, "Say that three times fast."

"How was your dinner last night?"

She had leaned in close, as always, to make sure she heard me. Now she sat back, smiling. She always made me feel the importance of my words.

"You're right. Change the subject. Dinner was very nice. I had steamers for the first time."

"Ronny told me he had a great time. I never went out to eat except for certain bars at happy hour. It's a habit I fell into when I lived in rooming houses. To cook in the rooming house meant to clean up after yourself. I took to eating at happy hours—wings, nachos, things like that. Then I got the apartment."

"Ronny said you have a daughter, Alice, and two granddaughters. And you can't visit them?"

"Her husband doesn't allow me to visit their home."

"Why doesn't she come visit you?"

"Keep the peace. That's what I told her. She called me Monday, and I spoke to the girls. I call every Sunday. If I miss, Alice gives me a ring the next day. The girls haven't seen this," I pointed to my stoma. "Jessica's three. I'm just a funny voice to her. But Suzanne's five, smart as her mom. She remembers my voice from before the surgery."

"Why won't your son-in-law let you visit?"

"Please," I held up a palm. "History."

After our morning time together, Robin stayed by the stand talking to Ronny or spent time with her friend Lisa, the girl she brought to the Tropical that night. Lisa sat way down the beach from the stand.

I didn't stay much past noon. Almost July with the humidity right on schedule, even under my umbrella it was just too hot. I stood up to leave when

Robin came back from a stand visit. Ronny put on a shirt and grabbed his backpack.

"Going to lunch?"

Robin ran up. "Damn, that sand's hot."

"Benny feet," I pointed to my towel. She stood on it. "I'm going home."

"Okay. It is hot. See ya." She packed up her bag with her stuff and ran down to the stand. She dropped everything and then disappeared to her shoulders behind the tide rise. I could see her hair puffing in the breeze coming off the surf. Ronny walked down there with her, and the two of them headed south along the shoreline. I watched them go until they were out of sight, way past the Lake Pavilion.

There were die hards sunning near the boards—they had to be melting. I sweat pepperonis until I got home. I set the thermostat to February to cool the place down. I needed a drink of something and checked the fridge. A six pack of Pabst with one beer torn off, a few loose cans of Bud, and a half-full gallon container of iced tea.

I took a drink right out of the iced tea container. It tasted terrible. I checked the label—unsweetened. I decided to sweeten it. I poured in some triple sec and some vodka, shook it all up, and poured that into a tall glass with ice. The iced tea was Ronny's, but he was out to lunch by now, sitting somewhere cool with Robin.

I got on my radio, but nobody came back, so I got the turntable going. It had a stack of records already set, so I hit the switch. I got undressed and climbed in the shower with my drink. As soon as the music started, I knew Ronny must have replaced my records with his own that morning after I left for J's and the beach.

I stack my three favorites in order: *Smokey Robinson and the Miracles Greatest Hits Vol. 2*, the original Broadway cast soundtrack of *South Pacific* with Mary Martin and Ezio Pinza, and *The Four Tops Greatest Hits*. I didn't hear Smokey Robinson. I recognized Bruce Springsteen but not the song.

After I finished up in the bathroom, I came out and drums, guitar, and a red-hot piano froze me. The song was about a black Cadillac—a long, dark, shiny Cadillac. I heard the chorus and blasted it, and then I picked up the tone arm to start the song over. The needle skipped across the grooves. It made a hell of a racket. Water dripped from my hair onto the record while I tried to find the right song. The lyrics sat inside the two-record set titled *The River*, and I followed along. The chorus got me pumped.

Cadillac, Cadillac/Long, and dark, shiny and black/Open up your engines let 'em roar/Tearing up the highway like a big old dinosaur.

I picked up the tone arm again and played the song through a couple of more times. *Open up your engines*—damn, I liked that song. I played it while I stood out on the balcony and looked out at my car. I played it getting dressed.

Just for the hell of it, I drove to the local library to see if a place called Cadillac Ranch existed. The library is on Seaside. It's a Carnegie library. I remember going on field trips to it in elementary school.

I discovered that there is a place called Cadillac Ranch. It's near Amarillo, Texas—ten Cadillacs buried front-first. The latest model is a '63.

I told Mrs. Toner, the librarian, "Maybe if I drive mine down, they'll give me some money and make it number eleven."

"You drive a Cadillac, Jimmy?"

I just smiled at her. She's always kidding me. She told me once she sets her watch date by me because I always show up with my books or records on the due date.

"You're a single gentleman, am I right?"

"Mrs. Toner, that's why I can afford a Cadillac." I didn't tell her it was a '64. I bet she peeked out the door after I left, though.

Driving home along Ocean Ave, the northbound traffic stopped. I looked ahead, saw the men on the Inlet Bridge come out of their gatehouse, and walk the gates shut. A few cars turned left and raced to the F Street Bridge to beat the fishers. I parked and got out.

I walked onto the beach just in time to see the fishers coming in, trailing one another in a long, wake-edged line. I could see the big-toothed gears that opened the steel grate halves of the bridge. The lead fisher passed underneath, its flying bridge and antennas stretching up, gulls screeching alongside. Wake slapped up against jetty rocks.

Up on the road people stood on the bridge walkway outside their cars, stretching and waiting. Some came to the concrete railing and looked down at the fast-moving water. I hadn't watched the fishers come in up close for years. Seeing it all made me feel young.

I didn't stay for the whole line of boats. Everybody must have booked a half-day. I bet the bridge stayed open ten minutes. There were a few big private boats, too. Sailboats with tall masts, one big yacht with a three-level bridge with big antennas on each side.

At home, I fixed myself a drink and found a ballgame—the Yankees in an afternoon tilt, as Red Barber would say. I spent a lot of afternoons on the beach listening to Mel Allen and Red Barber. Phil Rizzuto, too. Holy cow!

I settled in, nice and comfy. The afternoon flew by, and that jug container of iced tea did a poor job of keeping up with the 1.5 bottle of vodka. I don't know why I hit it so hard, but I did. The end of the game, me going into my room for a nap, and Ronny coming in from work all ran together.

He was noisy as hell. In the bathroom, in the shower, then out playing with the TV, then back blow-drying his hair. I got up, went in the bathroom, and after I pissed, I started picking up towels. There were towels all over the floor, across the sink, over the shower rod. I threw them out into the living room where he sat with a drink and a frozen dinner. I had one more balled up that I dropped at his feet.

"You see these towels? They're all your towels. How many towels do you need?"

I couldn't catch my breath. I went in my room and tried slamming the door, but it slid into some clothes on the floor and stayed open an inch. I fell onto my bed. Those little black spots swirled around on the ceiling.

I folded my hands on my chest and tried to relax. I did. When I woke up, TV light from the living room seeped through that doorway inch. Voices whispered. I got off my bed and moved to the inch.

"Look Linda. I don't feel like taking a ride."

"Ah, one favor."

"One favor for you, one jail term for me."

"We just need somebody to buy some beer for us."

I peeked out. Linda stood next to Ronny, who sat in the big chair.

"Tony says please."

"Is that so?"

She helped herself to one of his cigarettes. Then she took a sip of his drink.

"It's good." She helped herself to another taste. "C'mon, you can spare ten minutes."

"Driving with your bike in the back of the Caddy? Very questionable."

Her tummy was right in his face. "Please?"

"That's all I need."

He got up, went into the kitchen, and opened the liquor cabinet above the sink. I could just see him. He looked up when Linda came alongside. She stretched way up on her toes and pointed up at something.

"What's that?"

"Mezcal."

Her top lifted along with her arm. She stayed on her toes, leaning on him for balance.

"What's that?"

"Tequila. Very bad for little girls."

"That the one with the worm in it?"

"That's the one."

He brought down the bottle to show her. She tapped it next to the worm, then lifted it and looked through the bottle's bottom.

"Can I take this?"

"Hell, no," he hissed. "That's Jimmy's."

"Hey, while I'm here, can I have my dress? The one I left here?"

"It's in one of Jimmy's drawers. He's asleep."

"He doesn't like me."

"He knows you're trouble. That's the word for you—trouble." He took the Mezcal from her, reached into the fridge, and pulled out that six-pack minus one of Pabst. "Here, take this. There's even a convenient handle."

"What's the matter with you?"

Ronny went into the living room. "Go see your boyfriend."

She followed him. "I can't ride my bike with this," she held up the five-pack.

"I'll put it in a bag for you." Except he didn't get a bag. He flopped down on the couch.

"It's not that. I don't care who sees me. I can't carry it and ride my bike."

"Excuse me?"

She stood in front of him. She didn't move. He poked her bare stomach with a finger like a gun.

"You have your beer."

She sat down next to him.

"What?"

"What?"

They had their eyes on the TV. She sat at one end of the couch with her knees pointing toward him and an arm thrown over the back.

"I thought you were going. You have your beer, don't you?"

"I told you; I can't carry the beer *and* ride my bike."

"That's right. You did. Are you coming to the beach tomorrow?"

"Why?"

"Come to Inlet. Bring your friends. I'll get them on for nothing."

"They all have badges."

"I'll take you for a ride in the guard boat."

"Why do you want me to come to your beach so bad?"

"I want you to meet my girlfriend."

She popped two beers and gave one to him. "Can I sit here?" she patted the middle of the couch.

"I'm a little bashful."

"You, bashful? That's lie number two."

"What was lie number one?"

"Guys like you don't have girlfriends."

"How are you and your boyfriend getting along?"

"Tony? He's okay. He can be a real pain."

"How so?"

She swiveled around, drinking from her can, pouring it into her open mouth. "He's okay. Everything has to be his way, you know? He's his favorite subject. Tony, Tony, Tony. I can't *talk*—"

"*Shhh.*"

"I can't talk to anybody; I can't look at anybody. He was so pissed at you the other day, that day you—"

"I know the day."

She tilted her head to one side. "What's with you and Margaret?"

"Margaret?" he chuckled. "Your mother?"

"Are you going to marry her or something?"

He took his cigarettes out of his shirt pocket. His shoulders shook with a silent laugh. "What do you think? I don't know. I haven't thought about it."

"I bet you haven't." She belched when she said "bet" and covered her lips with three fingers.

"Happens to the best of us."

"Remember that bone we almost smoked that night? That time you kissed me?"

He lit his cigarette. Linda reached for the pack. She lifted it out of his pocket, took one, and lit it with his lighter. She rested her cigarette in the ashtray.

I felt so tired. I was on my bed when I heard Linda again.

"Slow poke."

Aluminum crinkled.

"I can't drink if you don't let go."

"Try to take it."

"It's going to spill if I do. It'll spill—"

I heard a splat.

"Now you've done it."

I dozed. I heard the apartment door close. Footsteps went down the stairs. For some reason, I remembered the ashtray and those burning cigarettes. I fell asleep before I could get up, look out, and check to see if a cigarette dropped from the ashtray onto the table or rug.

The next morning, I felt the sticky trail on the wall above the lamp where beer had bubbled down in foamy trails. Two cigarettes had burned all the way down to the filter. Their ashes sat in the grooves like little gray snakes telling me the two left together.

You should know better I told Ronny that first time he tried to buy booze from me. I told myself looking in the mirror after I cleaned out that ashtray.

I spent Thursday straightening the apartment, talking on the radio. I didn't go anywhere. I never considered going to the beach. Same for Friday, except I got the Caddy washed that morning. I didn't see tooth or nail of Mr. Hopkins.

On Friday afternoon they started coming. They pulled into driveways and gawked on the boardwalk; they swarmed streets and sidewalks like thousands of in-laws with bratty, loud-mouthed cousins. July's flavor of the month: Weekend Supreme.

19

OH, BUT FRIDAY night, a northeast wind rose up to celebrate the big weekend. It blew until the water swelled with a drunken bully's swagger. When I stood on my balcony Saturday morning, I could see the Mercer Ave lines bowing hard to the south, the water surging fast and choppy, the breakers foaming a hundred yards offshore.

If it looked that bad from the balcony, it sure as hell would be an adventure for the guards on the busiest weekend of the year. Casivette would have to decide if he wanted to piss off the local businesses and red flag the water or piss off the guards and let people swim. Those flags can be seen from the boardwalk, but the Bennys don't always realize there won't be any swimming until they've paid their money.

Highspire already had a guard in the water—Harris, the rookie guinea pig. Hooked to a line letting the current take him, he tested the strength of the run. His head bobbed around, arms cupping the water in front of him so he could surface dive at each breaker. It was one dive after another. He swept across the south rope, then out, but by the time they pulled him in, he'd been pulled much further south than offshore.

High tide had carved out a steep slope. The sand fell off right where the guard stand would usually be, dropped three feet straight down, and then leveled off to the wash. The choppy froth made Guinness mustaches wiggling and twirling with the wind.

Harris dipped his hair in the surf and whooped. He unhooked the line from his belt and belly flopped back into the swimming area. You'd think he'd just gotten laid for the first time, happy as hell, bouncing around out there.

He bounced out, walked up to the others by the stand, and shouted, "You gotta do it!"

"Was it that good?" Ronny smiled.

Harris puffed, "Uh-*huh*."

Ronny stepped down the ledge, well, slid down, and waded out. Out past the first barrel, the water swelled over his head. It ran so fast and the froth foamed so thick, it was difficult to keep him in sight. He dove under, swam crosswise with the run until he hit the south line, and then pulled himself out to the second barrel. Getting pushed all over the place, he let go of the line and let the run take him. He got out a few blocks down and came jogging back. Harris met him.

"What'd I tell you?"

"Whew. Goddamn." He caught his breath.

Harris ran past me.

"Coffee time!"

I walked down to the edge of the drop next to Highspire and Ronny.

"We have some beautiful water out there," Highspire declared, "for drowning." Vinny and Cooper stood in front of us in the backwash, watching the water. The spray lifting off the surface surrounded them in mist.

"No bathing today, Highspire," Ronny smiled.

"Waiting for the word."

He didn't wait long. The stand's phone rang. Ronny trotted back to the pole, answered it, came back, and announced, "It was Casivette. No bathing."

I walked back to my umbrella, sat down, and picked up my paper from under my thermos. Highspire ran past me up the beach to the locker to grab the red flag that meant no bathing.

Ronny followed him. "I'm going to give Annie a few lines in case somebody gives her a hard time about the flag."

I put down my paper. A chilly mist blew off the water. I decided to go across to J's for my own coffee and a hard roll. Benny gear passed me like it was noon. Coolers, beach chairs, baby carriages, umbrellas—all headed close to the water. Umbrellas—in that wind!

I talked with Annie at her gate when I got up there. Harris walked across the street with his coffee. He still had a towel wrapped around his waist. Highspire had gotten himself into a conversation with one of the beach regulars—a mother who wanted him to explain why her son couldn't go swimming. The kid looked about twelve. Highspire put his points forward; the mother countered with hers.

"He knows this beach," the mother claimed.

Knows this beach. I remember thinking, what possible difference could that make? A classic Thunderbird drove along Ocean Ave. It had a big, toothy front grill, and I wondered, is that a '63 or a '64?

The rest of the morning dragged. The lines at the businesses along Ocean Ave stretched long and far as people ate and drank their day away. I took a break from the sun and sat in J's watching the heat coming off the parked cars. By afternoon, the wind gusts slacked off. People took a chance and opened their umbrellas to get some relief.

Splashers filled the backwash. Standing ankle deep, they'd squat, splash, then take a step out and splash more. Gaining courage, some dipped their butts—not a good idea with the tide in. A few had to be pulled out. One old guy whirled ass over teakettle a good twenty feet before Ronny grabbed him. The guards didn't get pissed—they got even. They went swimming.

Robin never showed up, but Linda did, with two girlfriends and a gang of male worshipers who sat outside the Benny rope. They tried to out-curse each other while the girls hung around the stand.

Ronny sat up there with Cooper. He turned up the radio when he saw Linda coming.

"Hey, Ronny," Linda called up.

Cooper looked down and tapped Ronny's knee. "Somebody for you."

Cooper kept looking down at Linda as she talked. Ronny kept his eyes on the water. Guards talk on their perch as if nobody is around them, and Cooper is no different. He turned to Ronny.

"Who is this? She a friend of your nurse?"

"She is the fifteen-year-old you were ready to banish me for bothering. Your daughter was next, you thought. Remember?"

"Her?"

"Me," Linda stood on the stand's first step. She brushed the sand off the second step to make a spot for herself. She climbed up. "Okay if I sit here?"

"No," Cooper said.

"You're there."

She looked up at Ronny, squinting, and a hand over her eyes, smiling. "Where's your girlfriend?"

"Putting with a doctor."

"You can't be on the stand. Please climb down."

"Relax, Cooper." Ronny hopped down and turned around. Linda held out both arms to him. He squeezed her hips and guided her to the sand.

"Thank you," Linda said.

"Harris is back. Going on break, bros." Ronny spread out a towel behind the stand, stretched out, and covered his face with a T-shirt. He folded his arms King Tut style. Linda stood in front of the stand talking to Cooper and Harris—mostly to Harris.

"Where do you go to school?"

"Ask her out, Harris," Ronny lifted his head. "Never mind where she goes to school."

"What?"

"Ask her out."

"He wants you to ask me out."

"Okay. You want to go out?"

"Not with you."

"Oh, say you will!" Ronny sang.

The two girlfriends were in love with Harris. They stayed to talk to him, but Linda walked behind the stand alongside Ronny. She sat down, gathered a fistful of sand, and held it above him. Wiggling her pinky, sand spilled onto his chest. A little mound grew on his sternum.

"Okay, Linda."

"You're all sandy. Want me to brush it off for you?"

"Sure."

"Linda," called one of Linda's boy companions, a tall, skinny, pale kid with a scraggly goatee.

"What?"

"Linda."

"What do you want?" Linda half-brushed, half-slapped off the sand. Then she scrambled around behind Ronny and started rubbing his shoulders.

"I have to go to work. Bye," the skinny kid said. "I just wanted to say bye."

"Bye." She kept rubbing.

"Hold on," Ronny rolled onto his belly. "Work my back."

She leaned down, pressed her palms flat, and gathered his skin leaving red, sandy marks.

"You have a zit on your shoulder." She pinched it, brushed the spot. "Where's your girlfriend if she's not here?"

"I have no idea."

She trailed fingernails from the base of his neck down his spine to his tank suit, where she moved side-to-side, fluttering nails on the material. "You owe me, Ron."

He didn't say a word. For minutes, he didn't move a muscle. With a bored sigh, she slapped his butt, stood up, and took her gang south.

She was long gone when Ronny lifted his head to look around. He stood, brushed himself off, and went around to the front of the stand.

"Where the hell is Highspire, Vinny?"

"I hope he got in a bar fight and didn't' know nobody."

"What's going to happen with that girl, Hopkins?"

"I'll tell you, Cooper. We're going to elope and open a haberdashery."

Harris looked at Ronny. "A what?" His eyes moved from Ronny to Cooper to Vinny, and all three laughed at once.

20

HIGHSPIRE SNAPPED THE lock on the chain anchoring the boat and stand to the dead man.

"See you there, Jimmy. Fifth house on the left on Chester between A and B."

I knew the party's location—less than a block down from Peggy's house. During the Fourth, everybody's a high school freshman. Story lines play in your head before they happen.

I put a hand on Vinny's arm and asked him about the party. "I have to hear these things from Highspire now?"

"Ooh—you didn't know about it? I got the Mahwah girls here." He hurried up the sand after two girls. He looked like a demented stork. Both arms out, shoes in one hand, sweatshirt in the other, wet rowing shorts in his teeth. All three climbed into a bright blue Mustang convertible.

The beach cleared in a hurry. On the boards, I stood looking at the Ocean Ave traffic. Strictly stop-and-go. Across the street, people's steps hurried. Evening plans kicked into gear. I could hear summer telling me, *Jimmy, it doesn't matter if you're going north or south tonight. I'm packing them all—dance bars, fern bars, dive bars.*

Walking to the apartment, I couldn't remember when I last spent an entire day on the beach. Long shadows of the houses across Ocean reached the boards. The sun smacked right into my eyes.

Guess who was in the shower when I got home. I knocked on the door with the side of my fist.

"Jimmy! Needed a shower before the party."

"Sand down your ass?" He couldn't hear me.

"Harris is picking us up after he eats something."

What the hell. I wasn't going to confront him now. I was up for the evening. I opened the door and brushed back the curtain. "Save me some hot water."

We were both ready, waiting on the sidewalk for Harris to swing by when Ronny mumbled, "I'm starting to hear songs on the radio and associate them with a certain girl from Paterson. You know what? I could use something before this thing."

"Right. Just a shower doesn't do it."

We went back inside. Again, it had been years since I went to a guard party, so a bracer was called for.

Guard parties have a pattern. Guys arrive in small groups: a beach, a town, whatever. The groups split up, the kegs get emptied, and the groups get back together. Of course, now everybody's smashed. It's time for somebody to try to take up a collection for another keg or some cases. The banded brotherhood vanishes.

We'd had a screwdriver each when Harris pulled up out front and blew his horn between cymbal and snare beats. I stood on the balcony and waved him up. He got back ten minutes later after he found a parking space. I put on that Springsteen record, "Cadillac Ranch."

"Like that song, do you, Jimmy?"

I nodded. I played it once more, and then put on something else. When I looked around for my screwdriver and my voice, I only found my screwdriver. Ronny started to rush us out the door.

"We need to go. Let's go."

I took hold of his arm, pointed to my throat. "My voice, where's my voice?"

"What? Where's your voice?"

I could picture it next to my screwdriver, which had made a wet ring in the middle of the record jacket of *The River*. It had been sticking straight out from Bruce Springsteen's picture on the jacket's edge. I remembered thinking when I put it down; it looked funny that Springsteen had my silver, right-for-his-picture electrolarynx for a microphone.

I went into my bedroom to look. It wasn't there. There are only two places I put it down—on my night table in the bedroom, and next to the turntable. I had no idea what the hell could have happened to it, but I thought the hell with it. I had on my white jogging suit with a lightweight, red T-shirt underneath and a blue bandana tucked in a pocket.

"Let's go," I mouthed.

"Just a minute. We'll look for it. Harris, Billy. Help me look for Jimmy's voice."

Harris made a what-the-hell face, then remembered, nodded, and started looking under pillows, under the couch, underneath the kitchen table, for chrissakes. Ronny came off the balcony shaking his head. Then he picked up the phone.

I shrugged, "You calling lost and found?"

"Hello, is Robin there?"

I pointed to my room, like I was going to check it again for my voice. I went in and picked up the extension.

"I beg your..."

"This is Ron."

"Ah! The famous Ron. Well, famous Ron, like I told you, Robin's not here right now."

"Ah, okay. Tell Robin Ron called, and that he's looking forward to coming over and getting together."

"Ron called. He's looking...forward to..."

"Are you writing this down?"

"I don't want any confusion." She finished reciting the message. "Is that all?"

"Lisa, right? Tell me, Lisa, didn't we meet at Estel's?"

"We met at Estel's, although I didn't give you my number on a matchbook. Then we ran into each other at the good ole' Tropical Pub."

The one in line. I remembered.

"Yeah, that's you. You told me to fuck off."

"Ah I said take off. I wanted Robin and me to take off and leave that urine-soaked hole which you find so charming."

"That's sarcasm. A biting or cutting remark. Tell me, sarcastic Lisa, you are having a party over there tonight, right?"

I could hear a slew of voices in the background, laughing and talking over music. Lisa never spoke up again. She must have put the receiver down and walked away. The voices kept going—I recognized Lisa's—and then the line went dead.

"C'mon, Jimmy, let's go!"

I came out of the bedroom.

"The little witch."

"Who?"

"Lisa, for chrissakes. As if you didn't know. Fucking spy master."

Harris dropped us off at the guard party. We—Ronny—paid two guys sitting in lawn chairs at the end of the driveway to get in. One took the money, and the other stamped our hands with a red rooster or chicken, I couldn't tell.

This thing had been going on for a while. There was one empty keg tipped over in a washtub, bottles, and cans all over the sandy yard. The place had the usual Belmar postage-stamp front yard with back yards so narrow you could hear a fart two lots away. An old, single car garage anchored the yard's back property. The garage looked very tired. Tom Sawyer whitewashed it last. A double sliding door that hadn't slid in decades sat open on one end far enough to let two people at once pass in and out. Smoke of a familiar fragrance curled from it. Two slat windows above the sliding door made the garage face look like an old man's crooked yawn.

I spotted Vinny with his girls from Mahwah. Ronny and I went over. One of the girls was smoking.

"How about a light?" Ronny held a cigarette up to her.

"That's an original line."

Ronny smiled at Vinny. Vinny laughed.

"A friend of yours?" the smoker pointed.

"You didn't' see Hoppy today on the beach? This is Ginny, and this is Mary."

Ginny, the smoker, had very long legs with slim ankles. Auburn bangs framed green eyes, then lengthened and flowed past her shoulders. Mary popped right out of the Sunday comics—a Daisy Mae body with red, naturally curly, Frieda-from-*Peanuts* hair. They both licked their lips before speaking.

I checked out the food. It didn't look edible. It was help yourself to the dogs, burgers, and rolls, then cook your own on the two halves of an oil drum set up with grates and coals smoking like hell. Ketchup, mustard, empty tubs of slaw and potato salad all sat on a couple of middle-heavy card tables. The flies had long ago notified all relatives. A herd of red plastic cups lay on the ground around a single trashcan overflowing with food-stained paper products. Chinese lanterns hung from a rope stretching from the back of the house to the only tree in the backyard. An open second floor window filled with two speakers blared Oldies 101.1.

I lost Ronny, but I found an upright plastic cup, rinsed it with a garden hose, and drew a beer at the keg. It tasted good and cold. For the next, I don't know how long I never moved. I stood by that keg, pumping it and filling people's cups. I smiled and nodded you're welcome when they said thank you. I never drew myself a second beer.

Next time I spotted Ronny, he stood on the stairway leading to the back door. The stairway, five steps and packed at each railing, had a center lane that moved toward the porch and door. I figured it was the girl's pee lane since almost everybody heading into the house was a girl except Ronny. The guy standing at the top of the stairway, the same one who had stamped our hands, stopped Ronny with a palm on his chest. They talked a little, then two guards and a girl came up to the keg. I held out my hand for their cups, one at a time, and filled them up.

When I looked back to the stairway, I didn't see Ronny, or the guy he'd been talking to. I didn't think anything of it.

I had fun being beer tender until Peggy arrived. She looked right through me, a cigarette in her hand and a smirk on her face.

"Well, well. Look who's minding the beer."

I smiled with my mouth closed and nodded.

"I just saw that son of a bitch friend of yours."

I made the signs for I don't know. Nothing—she just stared. I fingerspelled Ronny. She didn't budge. "Who?" I mouthed.

"Never mind. Jesus. Have you seen Linda here?" She swung her head around, looking over the crowd. "I know she's here somewhere."

I shook my head no.

"Ah!" She turned and marched down the driveway, her legs rolling at the ankles from her cork platform shoes. She disappeared in a crowd, but I caught a glimpse of her turning left out on the street, walking with a purpose, I think the phrase goes.

For some reason I didn't consider pissing behind the garage like all the guards. I thought I'd get in that center lane on the stairway and wait my turn inside. Maybe I'd find Ronny. I passed Casivette heading to the house. He didn't acknowledge me. I got to the porch, went inside, and found the bathroom. What a disaster.

Outside again on the porch, I could look over the gathering, and I spotted Ronny in the driveway, at the end of it, standing on the sidewalk. He had that half-pint of vodka in one hand and a cop at the end of the other outstretched palm. The cop moved one hand back and forth, gesturing from the backyard to the street.

I knew the problem. You can't have an open container on the sidewalk or near the street. If you have a cup, fine. If you have an open can or bottle of alcohol, then you get fined. It's a dicey law. To be safe you need to stay on your front porch. If you're in the front yard by the sidewalk, the cops sometimes can be pricks. The town claims sidewalks are public thoroughfares. Maybe they don't want any collisions while walking under the influence.

Ronny had on his guard sweatshirt, so that was good for him because the cop would go easier on him than a Benny. Ronny handed the bottle over, and the cop poured out the vodka and handed the bottle to him before getting in his cruiser and driving away. I managed to get down the stairway and out to the end of the driveway.

I was going to warn Ronny about Peggy. I didn't have a chance because Linda got to him the same time I did.

"Jimmy, did you see my mom here? Ron, Margaret's here I think."

"Fucking douchebag!" Ronny drew a line with the toe of his sneaker across the end of the driveway even with the sidewalk. "Not here!" he drew another one three feet back, "Here!" He stepped on both lines with either foot. "Not here," he stamped, "here! Give me that." Linda had a can of Bud. He took it and went through the whole bit again. He slid one foot back and forth, then hopped from one line to the other, then did heel-toe-heel-toe, each time yelling, "Not here, here!"

The two lawn chairs that were at the end of the driveway were gone, but the guy who took our money came next to Ronny with his arms folded.

"Who are you?"

"Who the fuck are you?"

"I live here."

"You mean you *rent* here for the summer. *I* live here."

The rest of the conversation degenerated into "keep your voice down" versus "I fucking live here."

I didn't think either was going to do anything because the money taker kept saying, "You gave me trouble on the porch. Now this." He never unfolded his arms, and Ronny had to know Casivette had money invested in the party.

"Harris!" Ronny yelled.

Guards stood all around, hopeful for some excitement—a pep rally on beer and holiday adrenaline. "Hopkins, Hopkins," somebody kept saying.

Linda kept saying, "Calm down, Ron, calm down."

"I want you gone," the money guy said to Ronny.

"I'm leaving. I'm finding my ride."

Casivette had come alongside the money taker, and they spoke in quiet tones with their backs turned before Casivette faced around, "Take off, Hopkins," and walked away.

Linda pulled my sleeve. "Jimmy, my mother's been here, hasn't she?"

I nodded yes.

"Oh, Lord."

I stood there with Ronny and Linda, actors who'd forgotten our lines. I could not have spoken a word even if I had my voice.

Harris showed up.

"About fucking time." Now Ronny pulled my sleeve. "Let's go, Billy. We got another place to hit. Bye, Linda."

Linda called to Ronny, "You owe me, Ron. Big time."

"Your mother's looking for you, not me." With that, Ronny reached into the pouch pocket of his sweatshirt, took out my electrolarynx, and handed it to me as we walked to Harris' car. "I figured Peggy would show up. I didn't want you blabbing about Linda being at your place with me."

I turned on my voice. "You wouldn't trust gravity."

21

SUMMER MEMORIES ARE long term and short term. Decades later, people remember catching lightning bugs as kids, but after an hour, they can't remember where they parked. I was this close to calling it a night when Harris found his car.

"Where to?" he unlocked his door.

"Sussex, between A and B." Ronny lit a cigarette and blew the smoke out hard. "That bastard cop."

I hit Harris' shoulder and twisted my hand for him to turn down the radio. "May I suggest we stop at Huxley's first?"

"What the fuck for?" Ronny shot back at me.

"You won't mind what we bring out."

Harris looked at Ronny.

"Go ahead, stop. Make him happy."

Harris pulled into a space out back. I took him in with me. Inside, I told him, "I'll sponsor everything if you take a drive up to Asbury. Ronny needs to calm down before we hit this party."

"Okay with me."

I bought a bag of ice, two-quart bottles of Hawaiian Punch, a fifth of vodka, and a few packs of cheddar cheese Captain's Wafers. In the backseat I took the three bottles from the big paper bag and fixed up two party travelers by pouring out half or so of each Punch, and then adding ice and vodka. One for the front seat, one for the back—no cups—we drank right out of Punchy's own. Riding, the wind filling the car, we hit Ocean Ave and pulled forward to turn left.

"Where are you going? What happened to Sussex?"

"We're cruising. It's a holiday. Like a Sunday drive without church."

The radio played, the punch tasted great. The ride relaxed me. It didn't do much for Ronny, though.

Under Tillie's smile at the Palace Amusements in Asbury, Billy said, "Are we going somewhere?"

"To this Lisa's," I answered.

Nobody spoke again until Ronny spoke over the tires humming over the Inlet Bridge steel grating.

"Keep going to Barclay, Harris. No more fucking detours."

Billy drove toward the south end of town in stop and go traffic. Car lights started to blink on. White and blue clouds over the ocean shook hands. Bikes and skateboards passed between us and the cars parked along the west side of Ocean Ave. All the diagonal spaces on the east side were filled. People walking or jogging on the boardwalk didn't seem to notice any of it.

"I'll tell you where after you turn." Ronny read the house numbers.

"You said you knew where it was."

"Fuckin' relax, Jimmy."

"I'm relaxed. Are you?"

We pulled up in front. It was a cottage with a small front porch at the top of a half flight of steps. People crowded the porch—mostly girls with a few guys. Their talk and music from inside the house floated down the street. They spoke in soft tones to each other the way people speak during a play intermission— with a sense of privacy, yet at the same time with an interest in what others are saying. It sure as hell wasn't a guard party.

We parked blocks away—this time I took note of the surroundings. I stopped at the walk and swept my arm toward the place, showing the boys in. I stayed a few steps behind them. As soon as we hit the porch, Lisa met us.

"What's that you have?" she pointed at Ronny's punch. She sounded like a cop. She wasn't the frightened girl from the line at the Tropical.

"Lisa."

"Right."

"Well," Ronny held up the bottle, "this is Ron's Hawaiian Punch. It's looking forward to getting together with Robin."

"Hawaiian Punch. I bet."

I held out my hand to her, and when she took it, I turned it and brought it to my lips. "Nice to see you again." If the heads on the porch hadn't turned already—they did with that. Lisa smiled like she'd had a few belts.

"Hi, Jimmy."

"Excuse me, but as you know, I use this to speak to you. At parties I usually tuck it away because it can't be heard."

Lisa shook her head yes the whole time until Ronny took a step to move around her. "Whoa, there. That bottle needs to stay outside. There's some beer in the cooler, and some wine, but no hard stuff, and no funny cigarettes. This isn't our house to wreck."

Billy went inside.

Ronny put the bottle down on the edge of the porch behind the railing. "Happy?"

"Robin's still not here."

"How do you know I'm looking for her?"

"Because you just said so."

"Did you give her my message?"

"She hasn't been back to get it."

I almost stepped around him and went inside for a beer, but I didn't. Lisa stood right in front of him like a roadblock.

"The famous Ron."

"What's this *famous* shit all about?"

"You mean you don't know?"

"You know your problem? You never had your belly button kissed."

"Yeah, right."

"From the inside?"

People started pouring out of the house. It was a fire drill. Everybody squeezed onto the porch or spilled down onto the steps or front walk.

"What the hell's going on?" Ronny said.

I was two people away. I heard a voice say, "Saluting the hour. House custom. Every hour on the hour."

All the people wanted spots by the railing. Somebody with a watch counted, "Three, two, one, saludo!"

"Slainte!" I didn't have anything to drink.

Lisa spun past the crowd to stay between Ronny and the front door as people went back inside. Ronny stepped behind the last guy heading inside, and Lisa cut him off.

"What the hell?"

"I'm going to talk to you. I've been waiting for you to show up so I could talk." Her folded arms and her smirk told me she'd had more than a few belts.

"No thanks," Ronny said. "Can I get by for a beer?"

She backed up to the door and put her hands on either side of the frame.

"Fine. Dizzy bitch."

He turned around and made for his punch bottle, but she jumped ahead of him again.

"What the *fuck?*"

She shook her head. "No. Not till I've had my say." Ronny put one foot back to turn, but she reached out and grabbed his sweatshirt at the shoulder. "No! I want my say!"

He smacked her hand away, and she balled the other into a fist and swung. He leaned back, and she missed. She lifted her foot as if to kick. When he stepped back further, she came at him with two raised fists. He sprung forward, arms shooting straight like a two-handed chest pass. The heels of his palms popped both her shoulders, lifting her off her feet. She came down, staggered backwards, and flipped over the porch railing above his Hawaiian Punch.

I was very relieved she hadn't broken her neck when she yelled, "You're nothing but scum!" from the evergreen bushes. She stood up, squeezing her fists in front of her face.

Seconds later, Robin stood in the doorway, a bottle of the same kind of Chianti I served at the dinner party in one hand, and a corkscrew in the other.

Ronny looked from Lisa to Robin and then back to Lisa. He walked to the railing. "You set me up! You're some fucking team, you two!"

"Ronny!" Robin said.

"Let him go, let him go. Scum! You're scum!" Lisa said. Ronny took off, heading for Ocean Ave. Robin went down the steps to check on Lisa. People stood on the porch for a while before going back inside. It was just past nine o'clock, just about dark, on the Saturday of Fourth of July weekend.

Lisa and Robin came back to the porch.

"I didn't know he was coming. When did he get here? Why didn't you get me? I was in the kitchen opening wine for the salute."

"He pushed me. He hit me."

"He *hit* you?"

They disappeared inside. I got Ronny's punch. The hell with this, I thought. I sat on the steps and took a drink.

A few minutes later Robin came out from the buzzing inside. "Well, I think Lisa's going to press charges. Jimmy, are you okay?" She sat down next to me.

I took out my voice. "I'll be happy to testify. I'm very sorry about all this. Is Lisa okay?"

"Thank goodness. One shoulder hurts. That's it. I think she'll have some bruises. Jimmy, why? How could he do that?"

"He can't be happy," I wanted him there. Right there, so I could say, *why the hell can't you be happy?* I took a drink. The punch soaked my mustache and ran down my throat.

"Take it easy, you'll choke." She wiped my neck with a pulled down sleeve.

"You'll be all sticky. Thank you. Do you know where Billy is?"

She looked at me. "Billy?"

"Billy Harris. The lifeguard. The kid." I felt tired. The punch ice had melted. I held up the bottle and looked at it. A warm, sticky bottle in one hand, my voice in the other. "He's my ride." I poured out the rest of the punch. "I guess you won't be coming to Inlet tomorrow."

"I don't think so. No."

We went inside looking for Billy. Robin gave me a downstairs tour. I remember every detail of that little cottage. A small fireplace sat in the living room to the left as you entered through the front door. The stairs leading to the four rooms upstairs were on the right. Through the living room into the dining room—a good size, with a big table and chairs. The table had a light blue tablecloth underneath a protective plastic cover.

Then straight ahead to the kitchen, which had the stove, sink, and drain board on the left, the blue refrigerator dead ahead, to the left and next to the back door. On the oven door rack hung hand towels with blue and yellow seashells. The curtains on the top half of the back door had little white and blue striped lighthouses. Off the dining room were the bathroom and two downstairs bedrooms on either side.

We never found Billy. Robin gave me a ride home in her car. She wore glasses to drive. She drove a Honda Civic. She kept her hands on the wheel at ten and two o'clock. In the dim light of her dashboard, I noticed she wore a Claddagh ring on her right hand, with the heart facing outward, which meant her heart was open.

"I like your ring," I pointed.

"Thank you."

"I never saw it before."

"I don't wear it all the time."

"The heart's pointing out."

She smiled without showing her teeth and nodded yes.

"That's good. Are you Irish?"

She looked straight ahead. "Jimmy, Robin *Malloy*? Bet your sweet ass."

"That's good. That's perfect."

And she was.

22

O N THE SATURDAY night of Fourth of July weekend, I had consumed a screwdriver, one draft beer, and a few mouthfuls of warm Hawaiian Punch with vodka. After Robin dropped me off, I wasn't on the sidewalk long enough to fart. I climbed in the Caddy and headed south. Riding with Robin, I'd spotted two empty diagonal spaces across the street from Estel's, and one of them had my name in it.

I got a space and waited in line. I don't know how long I waited to get into Estel's. The place was smoke, noise, and confusion. I picked the right guy to get behind. He pushed his way to the bar, and a minute later, I had a beer. I looked around, and Ronny and Harris materialized at the far end by the service entrance. They spotted me and came over.

"Hey, Ronald. How's it feel to be the new Andy Kaufman? See any women you want to assault?"

He ignored me and looked the crowd over. "Begonias are on break."

"What's your story?"

"I decided to stop at my room at the Commodore. Vinny stuck a message on my door. Come to Estel's. I called and got my bartender friend. He gave the phone to Vinny. He said where the hell are you? We're all here. He wasn't lying. Coming here I nearly knocked over a skateboard kid clomp-clomping past me. I passed Chester where the guard party was, so I ducked down a block to check it out. All I found was Harris here. I need a beer." He pointed at me.

"I'm good," I held mine up.

"You're a lucky bastard to have us all, Jimmy."

A minute later, Ronny came back with two beers. He gave one to Harris. "Yeah, I checked the party. Not much to it. No more kegs, no more hot coals. Even the radio was dead. Two or three groups standing under one Chinese lantern. The rest got used as piñatas. I told Billy about Vinny's note."

"The line to get in here would have been a half hour wait."

"Except when there's a band and they move speakers and instruments through the basement entrance."

"All it took was a twenty," Billy pointed Ronny.

"The running bouncers who change kegs always appreciate it. Golly gee, Billy. We didn't get our hands stamped." Ronny tilted back his head and laughed loud enough to turn heads. "I fuckin' live here!"

I spotted Cooper and his wife, Denise, and made for them. They'd made nice-nice. They were all smiles, standing in the far corner of the bar right by the big picture window. Ronny joined us. He looked at Denise.

"How's the kid?" The Begonias were getting set to rip.

"Kids. We have two." Denise held up a backwards peace sign just as Peggy came out of the Gulls room.

Her eyes grew an inch taller when she spotted Ronny. Then she smiled and came alongside him. She pulled his ear down to her mouth, touched the side of his face, and guided his head down. Whatever she told him made him happy judging by his smile.

She took off for the bar, and Vinny appeared. Estel's was the goddamn transporter room on *Star Trek.* Ronny gave Vinny a smack on the forehead.

"Why the fuck didn't you tell me on the phone Peggy was here?"

"I said we're all here," Vinny laughed. "Hoppy, lighten up."

"Did she say anything about me and Linda?"

Vinny laughed no just as the Begonias roared into "Sugar Magnolia." Ronny jumped at the second chord. He stood in front of the band and sang to the lead singer…*heads all empty and I don't care…Saw my baby down by the river…*then grabbed the mic through the verses…*she's got everything I need…*the vocalist gave way to save…his guitar. Vinny and Billy next to Ronny…*She's a summer love for the spring, fall and winter…* Half the people in the place bouncing pogo…Peggy with a beer back from the bar spun into Ronny who held the mic and spun into her. *I take me out and I wander around…*Then everybody—*Sun-shine, day-dream…*the floor bouncing…*doo, doo, doo, walking in the tall trees…*Ronny spinning, knocking into and off people…people stepping back…and the lead singer claimed back his mic…

"Just little boys," Peggy yelled to Ronny, "you're all little boys!"

"How 'bout that!" the vocalist yelled at the finish, and the band, crowd, and floor came up for air. After a minute, Peggy leaned into Ronny.

"What are you up to?"

"I have no idea."

"Vinny tells me you were right down the street from me at the party, and you didn't even drop by."

"Ah, I'm not supposed to drop by, remember?"

"Oh, that."

"Vinny tells you." He looked right at Vinny.

Some suitor slipped between Ronny and Peggy, his back to Ronny, and started going to town with Peggy. Ronny stared down Vinny one more time and made his way to Highspire.

"I talked with Casivette," Highspire said.

"About?"

"About you."

"What about me?"

"About you sticking on for the summer."

"Just tell me, for chrissakes, Highspire."

"Okay."

"Okay *what?*"

"Okay, you're on for the summer."

Ronny let out a whoop. The Begonias went into "Mr. Charlie" as Ronny kicked a side of his sneaker down the shin of Peggy's suitor. Bouncers never drop their eyes that low.

The guy bent over and then sat down holding his shin. "Sonuvabitch!" he yelled over and over.

"You like champagne, Peggy?"

"What?"

"Champagne. I'm celebrating. No strings attached."

"Hopkins—"

"The sonuvabitch kicked me!"

"Let's go." Ronny looked at me. "Did you drive?"

I shook my head yes.

"Let's get out of here. Get us the hell out of here, Jimmy."

I was too sober for Estel's. I followed the two of them. Ronny pulled Peggy right through the crowd, sloshing beer all over. They got to the door. Ronny handed the bouncer his beer, squared Peggy's shoulders with both hands, and guided her out the door and across the street to the Caddy.

"Tessinger's, James." Ronny pulled Peggy into the back seat, and I started the car.

Uptown was a different planet. Walking into Tessinger's—the bar where Ronny and I picked up Cooper that day—felt like a sigh of relief from Estel's. We found stools. Across from us on the wall hung pictures of neighborhood softball and Little League teams hung—some from years and years ago. No jukebox. Above the rectangular bar sat two TVs tuned to Yankees and Mutts.

The bartender, bald and pleasant in his white shirt and black bow tie, looked like a high school principal.

Neither of my passengers had much business being in a bar. They weren't loud at first. Peggy instantly became the sweetheart of the place, which as usual was filled with ninety-nine percent locals, mostly older men, with an occasional wife or female companion.

Evidently, Ronny wasn't serious about the champagne because he ordered two screwdrivers. I had a beer. A cold bottle of Guinness—best moment of the whole night. Gerry told Peggy she looked very nice. She smiled and looked across the bar at some gentlemen.

Ronny poked her shoulder. "Aren't you going to ask the occasion?"

"I don't see champagne."

The champagne and I were both invisible.

"Yeah, well. Champagne on top of what I've had wouldn't go."

"Yeah? So what is it? I mean the occasion. Your big news about the beach?"

"You knew?"

"Sure I knew. Vinny told me. John Casivette told Highspire, he told Vinny, Vinny told me. You lifeguards are worse than parrots."

My two passengers temporarily lost steam. Ronny watched the ballgames. Peggy just stared. Then she started picking swizzle straws out from their holder and sticking one end into another. When she sucked air through her drink's straw, Ronny ordered two more drivers.

"Well, you're on the beach. That's good news. If it makes you happy, I'm happy. Is that it? Did I guess it? Or is it something else? What's next? You know, you have a lot of them stored away, you know that? Lie after lie after lie," Peggy laughed.

"That was it. No lie."

"No lie."

The bartender was standing on the other side of the bar fixing orders when Peggy got up. She pushed her barstool, caught her foot behind its leg, and stumbled. She pitched forward, caught herself, and then kept stepping slowly. The whole bar kept an eye on her as she walked to the lady's room.

The barkeep came over to Ronny. "Is she okay?"

"I'll ask her." A few minutes passed. The bar teetered on a high wire as Peggy came out of the bathroom and headed back to her seat. "Tessinger's wants to know. Are you okay?"

She looked around. "Yes!"

She didn't touch her second drink. She worked on her swizzle straws and made a crown made from them. She put it over her head, broke it, and tried to attach it around her neck. She rested it on her boobs, drummed the back of her hand on Ronny's arm, and said, "What do you think? Look at my necklace."

He didn't look.

She smacked his shoulder with a hammer fist.

"Christ!" he turned before looking away. "Stunning."

"You know, when I did the laundry Thursday morning, I got some clothes out of my hamper, and I took some from Linda's hamper, and then I went in Linda's room and picked up some things from her floor. And you know what? Her panties, one of her little panties, it smelled like semen."

Ronny kept watching the ballgame.

"I sniffed them to make sure. Now what I don't know is whose semen that was. I guess it all smells about the same. Would you know anything about that?"

People around the bar got very quiet. Ronny turned and whispered something to Peggy.

"Please," the barkeep said.

"Ejaculate. That's the right word. *Cum.* It could've belonged to Tony, that skinny, creepy little boyfriend of hers. Or maybe somebody else I don't know. Or maybe somebody I *do* know. She won't tell me. The child rode her bike somewhere Wednesday night, that's all I know. Her *bicycle!* Her goddamn *bicycle!*"

The barkeep wanted to call a cab.

"He drove," Peggy pointed to me. "He did. He drove his car." She got up too fast and headed over backwards, clawing at air. Ronny snagged her arm above the elbow and pulled. It turned her, and she kept going, bumped into him, and ended up two barstools down.

"Are you okay?" he laughed.

"Terrific, bastard. You *jerked* me ten feet!" She pointed at start-finish lines. "From there to here!"

She headed for the door, and he caught up to her and took an arm.

"No, goddamn it! No, you'll put me through a window. *I will have your ass!*"

She had an *Exorcist* voice. They rumbled out the door, him holding her up, her yelling and flailing as they hit the sidewalk just as a police cruiser passed. On went the cherry top. Many of Tessinger's patrons stood behind the blinking Bud neon in the window to catch the show.

Peggy gave them a good one. The cop walked up to her, and she flew into a story.

"We just got engaged," she wagged a finger from Ronny to her and back again. "We're window shopping for a dress for me to wear to the engagement party and have a disagreement." She marched down to Belmar Fashion Corner, pointed to a blue dress in the window, and told the cop, "I wanted that one, but *this* cheapskate won't spring for it."

I don't think the cop bought her act, but it was a young cop, and he didn't know Ronny, or else there's no *way* he would have let them go.

"I'm driving," I told the cop. "I'll get them home."

He watched as I pulled out and crossed with the green. I dropped off Peggy. She didn't say a word.

"You're not walking her to the door?"

"She's crazy, Jimmy."

"You fucked up big-time tonight."

"It's the boyfriend, Jimmy. I gave her some beer the other night. That was it. It's the boyfriend."

He repeated it twice more before I dropped him at the Commodore. Driving home, I asked myself why I bothered to follow him around. Was it because I wanted to look out for him, or wanted to see him fuck up? I was so disgusted with both of us I couldn't think.

That's part of summer, too. It goes so fast you want to sweep everything under the rug and let the dirt rest there until autumn. Sometimes we clam diggers forget all about the mess until somebody lifts the rug.

People were still out on the boardwalk—it wasn't even midnight. Hell, there was still a line at Estel's.

23

O N SUNDAY LOBSTER Bob, combo umbrella man-beach cop, watched his boy-slaves unload rentals at the Inlet gate with a look on his face that spelled h-o-t.

"Yesterday caught me by surprise. I ran out of decent umbrellas by noon. Today I dropped them all off," he told me. "All the ones I left in the yard yesterday need repairs or cleaning. Bent spindles, ripped canvas, seagull shit."

The two kids unloading the umbrellas looked beat. Inlet was the end of the line. They'd been at it since 5:30 a.m., before the cars started parking in the diagonals along the boardwalk. "Bob, where's the seashore breeze? This air's so thick."

"Go back to Jersey City. Catch your breeze up there."

"Seriously. What the hell do you do all day besides check badges?"

"It's not just badges. I bust people with alcohol, glass containers, and radios without headphones. Behind my reflectors, I have a license to leer."

He headed off to change into his beach cop outfit—white shorts, shirt and bucs—to do what he loved best.

It was a quiet day, Sunday. The water had calmed down, people swam freely. Kids ran plastic buckets and shovels back and forth from blankets to water. I didn't feel like seeing people after I talked to Max and said hi to Annie. I went across to J's for a paper knowing the Lipp was home sleeping off Saturday night. I didn't think of going to the beach.

I went home after reading my fat Sunday paper outside J's—the heat got to me, and the humidity made it hard to catch a breath. I got home, cranked up the AC, and took a nap.

I woke up at lunchtime. I fixed myself a sandwich—nice salami with fresh mozzarella. I took a shower and had a shave. I'm usually very careful shaving, but when I got out my mustache trimmer, I forgot to check to see if the little adjustable guard was on the trimmer end. It wasn't. I ran the trimmer across one side like I usually do. Off came a big strip of mustache. I had no choice but to trim everything the same length. Looking in the mirror, my mustache looked like a dirty shadow—ridiculous. I took the razor to the poor remnants and saw parts of my face that were strangers.

I got dressed in my favorite Hawaiian shirt, a button down with palm leaves, coconuts and parrots, a pair of nice shorts, and sandals. After walking two blocks to the Caddy, I kept the top up, opened the windows, and turned on the air until the interior cooled down.

When I pulled up in front of Alice's house in Sea Girt, the front door was closed. Sometimes when everybody's home, they keep the screen door latched and open the front door for fresh air, but since it was so humid, maybe they were keeping the cooler air in.

Alice had the house looking sharp. She had some Asiatic lilies blooming along the front beds, and two big pots of red geraniums, white impatiens, and purple fountain grass on either side of the front porch. Her front beds needed work, though—she had nothing but short annuals—petunias and begonias. She needed height—some perennials, especially a few tall ones—maybe tall phlox, coneflowers, or Shasta daisies.

I pulled up further along the curb so I could see the backyard better. The girls had themselves a new playhouse. It had steps up to a plastic log cabin, a slide coming down, and swings attached.

I didn't know if I should continue this surprise visit. I knew that once I turned off the Caddy, I would go through with it. I thought about heading into Sea Girt and calling from a pay phone to see who answered. Sunday was my day to phone, after all.

I told myself that today was an occasion. No drunken cab ride like the last few visits. This is a holiday. You haven't seen the Caddy, I could say. I just wanted to drop by, say hello, and show you the car. Perfect.

In the neighbor's front yard, a woman came outside on a John Deere and started cutting her grass. Why she needed a tractor for such a small yard was a mystery to me. She mowed back and forth. Every time she faced my way, she glanced up at me sitting in the Caddy.

On her next trip, I turned off the engine, got out of the car, and stood on Alice's sidewalk. The neighbor woman stopped the tractor and throttled it down. She got off and stared at me.

I'd left my EL on the Caddy's front seat. Dumb ass, I told myself. I held up one finger, turned to go back to the car, opened the door, and got my voice.

Naturally, I had to walk toward her to be heard, and when I started walking, EL in hand, I don't know if she saw a gun instead of my EL or just didn't like my face. She backed a few steps away toward the open garage door she'd ridden from not five minutes before, then turned and ran in.

I stopped and held out a hand, "I'm Alice's father."

The garage door closed.

I just stood there for a while waiting to see if she would return. Maybe she'd open the garage, come out, and blast me with a .30-06. If she tried it, I'd jump on her still idling, prized mower. I know tractor people. She'd never risk missing me and hitting her goddamn John Deere.

Alice opened her door. "Dad."

I smiled, waved, and came up her walk. "I'm afraid I frightened your neighbor," I pointed at the house.

"Who, Gloria? Never mind Gloria. You came for a visit? You shaved your mustache. Now you look like a retired gentleman."

"Lately, I've been kind of busy."

"That's good, Dad. You're getting out?"

"I go here and there."

"That's good." She glanced down the street toward the beach.

"How about this?" I motioned for her to come see the Caddy.

"That's some car."

We walked down to it. She got in and checked it out. While Alice sat in the car, the neighbor's garage door opened. She turned off her tractor and came over.

Alice introduced us. "Gloria, this is my Dad, Jimmy."

"Nice to meet you, Jimmy." She almost hid behind Alice.

I showed her my EL. "I'm not a Hawaiian hit man."

Alice looked one more time toward the beach. Gloria waved nice meeting you and went back to her Deere.

"I'm taking a trip in my new car. Down to Florida and Disney World."

"That's some drive."

"I'd love to take the girls there. Suzanne would love it. Jessica's probably a little too young, though. Maybe in a couple of years. Tell the girls hello," I said climbing in the Caddy.

"You just got here!"

"You keep looking down to the beach."

She looked down the street one more time and then back at me. She huffed out a breath as if blowing out a single birthday candle. "Bill took the girls for a walk."

"And they're due back."

"Yes. Dad—"

"It's best. No sweat. This was much nicer than a phone call."

Alice leaned on the driver's door with both arms. "I'm glad you stopped by. Any reason?"

"I don't know. I just wanted to tell you about my trip." I started up the Caddy. "Goodbye, honey. I'll send you a postcard with Goofy on it."

"I'm glad you came by. Take care. Call me, Dad. Promise? When you get there. Where are you staying?"

"Say hello to the girls," I waved.

Driving home, the beach traffic was ridiculous, so in Spring Lake I cut up through town. Since I was in the neighborhood, I stopped at Tessinger's. Gerry was working an afternoon-after-closing double. I remember working those.

He made only one comment about the previous night. "I couldn't believe those two."

"Well, I could."

There's something about being in a cool, blinds-drawn, dark-wood bar on an afternoon that's hot, humid, and bright. It's not just the booze or the beer. It's peace, civility. If there are one, four, or eight other people, they're all your friends. You're all in there together; you might discuss sports or politics. Everyone will be civil. They'll talk to you like a neighbor. That is exactly what they are at that moment. On a barstool, next to you. On that bright, sunny afternoon, if they had a better place to be, with people they loved or who loved them, they would have been there.

A man I didn't know asked, "How did you learn to speak with that? What is that gizmo called?"

"Electrolarynx. EL for short. I just call it my voice."

"I can't imagine what that would be like. It changed your life, I'm sure. You're to be congratulated. Tell me, why does it make that noise before you speak?"

"Even Sinatra taps his microphone."

Nobody ran back into a garage or stared at me without speaking. I had a fine time in Tessinger's. The afternoon ended along with Gerry's shift. As evening began, we shared a story before he went home. One by one, my afternoon friends left. They went outside, blinked back the sunlight, felt the heat lifting off the street blacktop. The lucky ones climbed in a hot car, rolled down the windows, and blasted the AC on their way through Sunday traffic.

There were fireworks scheduled for 9:00 o'clock in Asbury. I could either fight the traffic to drive up there or walk to Mercer Ave beach and watch them trail up, explode, and then, carried on a northeast breeze, hear a faint pop.

I stayed put on my balcony. I kept thinking about Linda's goddamn bicycle. Sky-blue, with white streamers. Peggy stated her child had ridden it somewhere Wednesday night. I looked down at my sidewalk. That was where she rode it, all right.

24

TOO FUCKIN' BRIGHT out here," Vinny tipped the stand forward while Harris dug in the two back legs. "The sun needs a dimmer switch."

"Dig deep," Ronny said. "I need a lot of lean today."

The water looked much calmer but dirty scum floated in long trails like boundary lines twisting out past the breakers. Cooper and Highspire ran the boat down. There was still a sharp drop along the tide rise because of Saturday's rough water. Just for the hell of it, I asked Highspire if somebody could take me out in the guard boat.

"I've never been out in one."

"I'll take him," Cooper said.

I looked at Highspire. His mouth gaped; forehead creased. He checked around. I didn't see anybody on the beach except some sleepers.

"On the Fourth? I was across the street, Cooper. It's on you."

Another cancer favor. What had it been, a week since the big fib? What the hell. I wanted a ride.

Cooper insisted I have a torp. I sat in the bow. Cooper timed the breakers, and Vinny and Billy pushed off. Cooper stood upright, one foot in front of the other. I'd seen him row—an outstanding oarsman—better than Highspire or Ronny. He took short, choppy strokes at first to beat the break, then out into the calm with longer strokes, the blades feathering and then cutting the surface again with barely a splash.

"Keep our stern locked on something like a house. Anything big enough."

"The old Lawson house on Ocean Ave."

"You brought your voice, huh? I know it. Keep us on it."

Peaceful doesn't begin to describe my ride. If we started drifting one way, I motioned a hand toward the other, and Cooper would leave an oar out of the water for a stroke. I leaned back listening to the water lap against the boat. Sunlight coming off the water beamed hot all around me. We were a good two hundred yards offshore when Cooper sat down with his back to me, sweat running from his shoulders. Then he started some serious rowing.

He rowed due east. The oars cut the surface, twisting in the locks until the Lawson's, the beach, and all the buildings along Ocean Ave melted into the water. When he leaned back and shipped the oars, the boat drifted and bobbed. Only the Inlet Bridge and some high-rise condos up north stuck out. Four sides of ocean surrounded us.

It wasn't like being on a big fisher. I've done that dozens of times. I felt close to everything. The hard seat, the gunnels in my hands, all the time feeling like a leaf on the dark green water. To tell the truth, after I stopped remembering Lawson's, I noticed how far out we were. It frightened me.

At the same time, though, I felt exhilarated! Do it sometime. Get a small craft, row out so the only sounds are the oars cutting the surface and working in the locks along with a faint, steady lapping under your bare feet. Then stop to take everything in—how tiny and insignificant you are.

"Wow. It's something out here, Sam."

It wasn't long before Cooper directed, "Take the stern. Guide me toward the Inlet Bridge, Jimmy." The boat jostled side to side with my weight as I moved from the bow. I didn't tell Cooper, but that scared me shaky. I might as well have been on a high wire.

After a few minutes, I thought I could see the guard stand on Inlet. It floated on the bright surface of the water. Then I saw that I'd picked out the second-floor balcony of a house. Landmarks were recognizable by the time Cooper, his Speedo-covered ass in my face, stood up and rowed us in.

Billy waded out with Vinny to escort us. We didn't need them. Catching a wave, Cooper dug in an oar or two to keep the boat straight, I put both hands on the transom, and we rode all the way to a spinning stop on shore. I didn't get my jogging suit wet.

Vinny, Billy, and Cooper had the boat over the tide rise and turned seaward when Highspire came back from J's. As soon as he settled on the stand, Vinny went up to the storage locker and brought down the costumes for the Fourth.

It's a great day for spotting red, white, and blue. People's suits, hair, you name it. Everybody's on vacation and primed to do ridiculous things. The guards wanted to look ridiculous to piss off Highspire.

They dressed right on the stand for maximum public embarrassment.

Vinny was the Statue of Liberty. He had a plastic replica of the statue's crown, a white sheet draped like a toga over one shoulder, and a dictionary to hold. He had a box of sparklers, and occasionally, he lit one, stood up, and posed.

Cooper wore a white wig, a three-corner hat, and held a bag of cherries— red grapes—along with a toy hatchet. He had a multi-stemmed, potted plant, and when Vinny lit a sparkler, Cooper pretended to chop.

Ronny topped them both. He sat between George and Lady Liberty decked out in his over-sized Yankee hat; white, stapled paper cuffs; an actual pair of red-stripe pants; and a cotton van dyke stuck on his chin. He'd point at passersby, "Uncle Sam wants *you*!"

The three got smiles and stories from the Inlet faithful and a disgusted look from Highspire.

The morning flew and the afternoon heat started cranking big time. Flies rode an offshore breeze from F Street to the prime pickings on the sand. By noon, I'd about had it. I put my umbrella and chair into the guard locker, gathered up my blanket, and went around to the front of the stand with every intention of saying good-bye for the day, maybe for the summer. Anything could happen in Key West.

Ronny wouldn't look down at me. The others all waved except old stone face. I looked up at him one last time, and I noticed the sky inland. I hit his foot and pointed.

"Take a look west, Tecumseh." Everybody looked.

"Oh, baby," Vinny beamed.

"Ladies," Ronny said, "we might just be starting the tournament early."

"Highspire won' let us leave early on the Fourth."

"Offer a sacrifice to Thor." Ronny looked down at me. "How about being a sacrifice?"

I shook my head, smiled, and kept pointing my finger back up at the boardwalk, at my apartment, or at the sky. My other digits joined the pointer and flapped goodbye. Up at the gate, I talked to Annie for a good ten minutes.

"I'm concerned with the approaching weather."

"You'll be able to watch your shows." I told her I'd see her soon even though I knew I wouldn't.

I had everything I needed in the trunk of the Caddy except what I call my care satchel. Robin suggested that I have a basic care bag so that I always know where everything is. I even packed my new EL—the one Ronny bought me after kicking the tray table off the balcony. That seemed like ten years ago. I had to take breaks between trips out to the car.

I could hear faint rumbles inland. It was coming, but the Ocean Ave traffic didn't care. Neither did the bicyclists, skateboarders, or people carrying more crap toward the beach than I had in my trunk. Holidays make fun demons of us all.

Holiday or no, I had myself a nap. I fell asleep thinking about what stuff I'd packed and what stuff I might have missed. My mortgage was all set through August, and the electric and phone bills for July were paid.

A rip of thunder that sounded like it was having a beer on my balcony jarred me awake. I went out to there to catch the stampede—a human tsunami. Old couples, parents with kid playpens and kid tents, teenagers on bikes, it didn't matter, they all moved with dogged acceptance. Across the street, the dance bar parking lot was packed. The attendants hunkered down under their umbrella at the entrance.

Then the rain started. People who had paid for the privilege of bathing in the ocean now avoided getting wet for free. They ran like hell. I had an urge to run across to the dance bar. There would be some kind of drinking going on in that place even on the last day of the long weekend. It was, after all, the Fourth. I stayed put on the balcony and watched the show.

Déjà vu—Peggy coming here during a rainstorm, or just when it was starting to let up. I got the hell off the balcony and pulled the drapes. The shakes hit my fingers, and I turned down the AC. Even though it was a holiday, there was nothing but the usual weekday fare.

25

I WAS WATCHING TV, drinking chocolate milk, and eating shredded mozzarella out of the bag when Ronny came up my steps.

"How long are you going for?"

I didn't answer. I got up, went into my bedroom, and started sorting through things, things I knew I wasn't taking. I started pushing hangers aside in the closet. Next thing I knew, a fat booklet of travelers checks fanned in front of my face. Ronny gave me a big smile.

"How about taking me with you?"

I stared at him. "You come along; you're not getting your way. That's all."

He ran water in the sink and splashed his face. "Let's leave tonight. It's time for a change."

I laughed so hard I had to clear my stoma twice. I was still finding sand in the wrong places.

"With you—always. You change more than any guy I know." I looked at the floor. I shook my head. "Okay, I'll be your ticket. Get packed. Take the Caddy and go clean out the Commodore." He didn't waste a second leaving.

I picked out Dion's *Greatest Hits* featuring The Belmonts and put on "The Wanderer" knowing how many times I'd wandered the needle on that cut. I memorized every skip, pop, and scratch. I did something I hadn't done in over nine months. I got out my old sing-along microphone and its speaker.

By the second time around for "The Wanderer," I was all set. I had my EL in one hand, the mic in the other, turned up full blast, and I went downtown. What a god-awful racket.

I waited for a half hour. No Ronny. I kept looking for the Caddy coming north. The streetlights along the boards came on. Everybody walking, riding or even jogging seemed in no hurry except me. With the top down, Ronny came around the corner, double-parked, and hit the horn. I stood up on the balcony, looked down and held up my hands.

He got out holding a six pack.

 I nodded.

He came upstairs with the Caddy still running.

"Where were you?"

"Remember the girl bartender in the Engine Room? She was just getting off when I got there. I told her I'm leaving for Florida, and she goes, oh, no! We had some good-bye drinks before we went up to the room. Couldn't make me a bad person. Anything else? I mean anything else to take?"

"No. I'm driving first." He looked around the place as if he'd never been in it before. "What are you looking for?"

"Something I'll miss."

"You left that back on Sussex."

"I didn't know I was going to be doing this until an hour ago. I didn't know there was a fucking schedule."

"No schedule. Just a big blank calendar. Like summer. When did banks start opening on Sundays or the Fourth, Mr. Travelers Checks?"

"Triple A sells them."

"You got them last week. The expedient thing to do." After all the delays, I locked the apartment, went down to the Caddy, and got in. Ronny slid in next to me and popped open a can of Pabst from his six pack.

"It's not that cold." He gulped it down and popped another one.

We were almost at the Turnpike when Ronny started to belly ache about having to piss. He made me pull over, and I let him hear it when he got back in.

"This is the selfish kind of shit I'm talking about."

Smiling, he reached over, took my voice, and stuck it in the glove compartment.

"What?" I mouthed.

"Never mind. Just drive. You got me. Now sit back. Enjoy! Hit the Turnpike, then straight down 95. I know you have the new EL. I want to practice. Watch."

He turned on the Caddy's overhead map light and put a hand in the beam. He started to fingerspell. I couldn't make it out. I shook my head and held up my hands.

"I'll slow down."

He fingerspelled *Jimmy. Sorry I doubted.* "When I took your voice."

I didn't know what to say. I kept my eyes straight ahead and composed myself, and then I spelled back to him *good letters. You practice.*

Thanks. Yes, he spelled. "On the stand and with Katie at the Engine Room. You never missed your book." He fingerspelled *Jimmy to Disney World.*

We didn't rush driving down. We stopped early on the Fourth—the traffic sucked, and we were both shot. Next night, we stopped in Virginia, and then the next in Duck to see my friend, Albie, even though it was out of the way. After that, we made good time.

The Florida beaches weren't my favorite. The sand felt soft and glowed white; the ocean was like a lake—calm and warm. And the heat—bejayzus as they say in Ireland. We spent three days at Disney World, which impressed the hell out of me, especially Animal Kingdom.

At the Italian pavilion at Epcot, I saw the most beautiful woman in the world. She had long, coal black hair with green eyes, and she looked at me the same way she looked at Ronny and everybody else.

We got to Key West where we were the Bennys—the Tourons, they called us. Ronny tried to find a bartending gig to meet women. I got hold of Alice. She'd been getting my mail, and she had my disability check for July.

 Ronny acted differently from home. He didn't get pissed off as much. He behaved. Maybe because he was the visitor now, the guest. Every impression is a first impression. He wore a white hat.

He mentioned Robin a few times—I didn't contribute to that conversation. I suppose I should have told him the truth that the cancer wasn't back, but living with that idea, that it could happen, helped me appreciate my good health and new sights.

I loved telling people we met about Annie, Vinny, and all the rest. I missed seeing them. I missed my apartment with my radio, my music, and Alice's mural. I sent her, Jessica, and Suzanne Mickey Mouse ear hats.

I sent Alice the motel's address. I figured she could send me my check—I didn't feel good about Ronny paying for everything—and maybe a letter or postcard. I sent Alice, Jessica, and Suzanne postcards during the trip. I made one that read *Missing You*. If postcards say anything, it's usually *Greetings From* or *Hello From Beautiful* something or other. I got a blank postcard, glued on a picture of their house from my album, and wrote *Missing You in Belmar, NJ*.

I knew they lived in Sea Girt. They got the card.